Fugue

by

Lee Thuna

SAMUEL FRENCH

FOUNDED 1830

NEW YORK HOLLYWOOD LONDON TORONTO

SAMUELFRENCH.COM

ISBN 978-0-573-66261-4   Printed in U.S.A.   #7958

**IMPORTANT BILLING AND CREDIT
REQUIREMENTS**

All producers of *FUGUE must* give credit to the Author of the Play in all programs distributed in connection with performances of the Play, and in all instances in which the title of the Play appears for the purposes of advertising, publicizing or otherwise exploiting the Play and/ or a production. The name of the Author *must* appear on a separate line on which no other name appears, immediately following the title and *must* appear in size of type not less than fifty percent of the size of the title type.

FUGUE premiered at the Long Wharf Theatre in New Haven, Connecticut on March 28,1986. The production was directed by Kenneth Frankel, with sets by David Jenkins, costumes by Jess Goldstein, and lighting by Judy Rasmuson. The cast was as follows:

MARY . . . . Barbara Barrie
DANNY . . . . Richard Backus
MOTHER . . . . Rebecca Schull
ZELDA . . . . Peggy Cosgrove
OLEANDER . . . . Jess Osuna
NOEL . . . . John Bowman
KRU . . . . Alexandra O'karma
TAMMY . . . . Laura White

FUGUE was next produced at Syracuse Stage in Syracuse, New York in1988. The production was directed by Arthur Storch. Barbara Barrie and Tony Plana played the leading roles.

The third regional production of *FUGUE* was in 1993 at the Cleveland Play House in Cleveland, Ohio. The producction was directed by Arthur Storch. Barbara Barrie and William Atherton played the leading roles.

CHERRY LANE THEATRE

Angelina Fiordellisi, Artistic Director
James King, Managing Director

presents

FUGUE

A Play by

LEE THUNA

with

ARI BUTLER   CHARLOTTE BOOKER   LILY CORVO
LIAM CRAIG   DEIRDRE O'CONNELL
DANIELLE SKRAASTAD   RICK STEAR   CATHERINE WOLF

et Design	Costume Design	Lighting Design	Sound Design
Neil Patel	**Gail Cooper-Hecht**	**Pat Dignan**	**T. Richard Fitzgerald** **Carl Casella**

Music	Production Stage Manager	Technical Supervision	Casting
Stanley Silverman	**Scott Pegg**	**Aduro Productions**	**Deborah Brown**

General Manager	Public Relations	Associate Producer	Consultant
Roger Alan Gindi	**Keith Sherman and Associates**	**Martin G. Thuna**	**Jules Ochoa**

Directed by

JUDITH IVEY

Major support for Cherry Lane Theatre has been provided by:
Carnegie Corporation of New York, Cordelia Corporation,
Educational Foundation of America, Jerome Foundation,
Paul, Weiss, Rifkind, Wharton, Garrison LLP,
Harold and Mimi Steinberg Charitable Trust, Williams Family Foundation

Cherry Lane Theatre is supported in part with public funds from:
New York State Council on the Arts, City of New York Department of Cultural Affairs,
Council of the City of New York

NYSCA

NYCULTURE

www.cherrylanetheatre.org

CHARACTERS

MARY - Between 45 and 55. Must be both comedic and dramatic. Suffering from a rare form of amnesia, she is very vulnerable and at times, combative. Often spacey and just as often, keen and perceptive. She is onstage for almost the entire play. Enough physical appeal for a young doctor to be smitten by her.

DR. DANNY LUCCHESI - Probably 30 to 35. Attractive but doesn't give much thought to his appearance, which could be fairly rumpled. From a lower middle-class background, so in spite of his name, he could be African-American, Hispanic, Asian. And Italian. Extremely intelligent, bright, fast-thinking, intuitive - but suffering from his own inner demons, which have prevented him from becoming the top psychiatrist he is obviously capable of being. He has a lightness to him, a cover-up for his emotional turmoil.

MOTHER - 70's, though in some scenes she is in her fifties and sixties. Cheerful, ebullient, a working woman most of her life, so she's a bit more worldly than the stereotypical "mother". Born in Vienna, speaks with a very slight accent, mostly substituting V's for W's. Devoted to her daughter and granddaughter and very protective of them.

NOEL - 17. Thoughtful, introspective, caring, sweet and soft-spoken, far from a rowdy beer-swilling, pot-smoking teenager. Hardly a goody-goody, but because he is well loved by his wealthy family, he is secure and comfortable in his own skin. Dresses carefully and neatly but without much flourish. Capable of deep feelings, especially his love for the young Mary.

LIZ KRUGER - mid-twenties to mid-thirties. In excellent shape, eats well, exercises regularly, probably a runner. Very attractive with a natural sexuality. She has a strong, positive attitude, easy smile, easy manner. She wears good clothes, expensive, sporty and tailored. Comes from money.

ZELDA - Same age as Mary. They are contemporaries, childhood schoolmates, but that's as far as the comparison goes. Zelda is a bit loud, a bit coarse, could be a bit overweight, dresses pretty much the way she sounds. She is clever and clever enough to keep that part of her hidden.

TAMMY - In the course of the play, goes from about eleven or twelve to seventeen. A darling girl, shy, quiet, polite, but not cloying. As she gets older, she gets more independent and more demanding. She is very pragmatic, calling the shots as she sees them. She doesn't understand the nuances of hidden agendas.

DR. JOHN OLEANDER- A couple of years older than Danny, but infinitely more serious, dignified. He is also humorless, failing to get any of Danny's jibes, which endears him to Danny. Oleander is old money, could easily live on his inheritance. His choice is medicine and he is a hard worker, dedicated to his profession.

ACT ONE

(Chicago. Today. MARY'S ROOM. It looks more like a studio apartment than a hospital room. A bed with some cushions on it. A small table with some chairs around it. An armchair and an ottoman. A telephone sits on the small table next to it. Along one wall is a small kitchenette, a sink, stove, cupboards and small refrigerator. There are a couple of doors along the back wall, leading to closets and to Mary's memory. The door to the room is down left. It is always locked. Mary is in the room. She is a very interesting-looking woman – interesting because it is very difficult to pin-point anything very specific about her. She seems taller than she is because she is thin. Her hair is short – recently cut – and it's hard to tell if it's been combed recently or not. Either way, it looks fine. Her age? Well, she could be in her middle thirties. But if she told you that she was forty-five, you might look again and say, yes, she could be forty-five. Or more. One reason is that she has no gray in her hair and her face is unlined, unwrinkled. And again, she is thin. Today, she is wearing a clean white short-waisted blouse and a navy blue skirt and loafers. Later she will wear slacks or jeans, sometimes a sweater or another shirt, a jogging outfit. The clothes will be strictly functional, devoid of accessories and with barely a nod to style. However, this simple wardrobe makes her seem more vulnerable.)

*(AT RISE: There is a knocking at the door. The door is opened and **ZELDA** enters. Zelda has some gray in her hair – or they are blonde tips that look gray – and some lines on her face, some obscured by make-up. She always dresses as though she's on her way to a lunch date.)*

ZELDA. Cele!

MARY. *(same inflection)* Cele!

ZELDA. I knew you right away!

MARY. Ah.

ZELDA. I thought you might look different. But you don't. You don't look any older. You don't have any gray in your hair. See, I'm getting gray already. It's premature, of course. Remember my mother was all gray by the time she was thirty-five?

MARY. No.

ZELDA. You don't remember my mother was all gray?

MARY. No. And I don't remember your mother.

ZELDA. *(astounded)* You don't remember my mother?

MARY. No. And who are you?

ZELDA. Me? Me? Who am I? I'm Zelda! *(looks at her)* Don't you remember me?

MARY. No. *(beat)* What did you say your name was?

ZELDA. Zelda.

MARY. Zelda what?

ZELDA. Zelda Sterling. We went to school together – all through school, from the from the time we were six right up till the very end of high school!

MARY. Is Zelda Sterling your married or single name?

ZELDA. *(getting annoyed)* What difference does it make, Cele? You knew me all your life! I thought the minute you saw me, it would all come back to you.

MARY. Well, I'm sorry… uh… what did you say your name was?

(The light goes on behind the mirror. It is a two-way mirror and now it becomes a window. Behind the window is the second playing area, an office. Mostly an indication of the doctors' office, with a couple of chairs, maybe a table. In the office are DR. JOHN OLEANDER and DR. DANIEL LUCCHESI. OLEANDER is clean-shaven, neat, crisp. He wears a gleaming white coat over his starched shirt and dark trousers. He holds a clipboard with papers on it. DANNY is about thirty and

*in contrast to Oleander, vastly informal. He wears jeans
and a casual open-necked shirt, maybe a jacket. Maybe a
beard. Today's doctor.)*

OLEANDER. We call her Mary Smith. She is Caucasian, intelligent, articulate and generally in good spirits. Her age
is somewhat difficult to ascertain. Her hair isn't gray
and her face is unlined...

DANNY. What? Me worry?

OLEANDER. *(turning to him)* What?

DANNY. Mad Magazine. You know. **(OLEANDER** *doesn't know)*
The logo. The imbecile who says, "What? Me worry?"

(Oleander still doesn't react. He is fairly humorless)

In other words, why should she worry? She can't
remember anything to worry about.

OLEANDER. *(he doesn't get it and he doesn't care)* So?

DANNY. Forget it.

OLEANDER. Her physical condition is quite good, with two
exceptions. Her appetite is sporadic and extreme.
She'll either forget to eat at all – or she'll exhibit a
voracious appetite and eat continuously for hours.

DANNY. Forgetting that she has eaten.

OLEANDER. Possibly. The other condition is her feet. They
are blistered and swollen, with almost every kind of
podiatric affliction – corns, calluses, warts... ailments
that give every indication of...

DANNY. Tight shoes.

*(**OLEANDER** simply looks at him. **DANNY** gives up)*

Sorry. Fugue?

OLEANDER. They had her at Cook County General for three
weeks. When she was first picked up, her feet were so
badly swollen, her shoes had to be cut off. Her inces-
sant and compulsive wandering leads us to diagnose
her condition as fugue with residue of transient global
amnesia.

DANNY. With naturally no explanation.

OLEANDER. With naturally no explanation. There's no trace of drugs or alcohol in her system. Other possibilities are physical trauma, although there are no scars around the head or neck. More likely, emotional trauma. And possibly Alzheimer's. Could be any one of the three.

DANNY. Or all three.

OLEANDER. Or all three. *(closing the folder)* So look, I could set you up in an office and you can study her to your heart's content.

DANNY. Well, thanks, but no thanks.

OLEANDER. *(great surprise)* You're turning me down?

DANNY. What is this? You call me, you say it's urgent, I see you – because you found a woman wandering in the streets? Come on.

OLEANDER. Fugue, Danny? A real live, probably long-term amnesiac? Right in front of your eyes?

DANNY. Yeah. It's the real live that turns me off.

OLEANDER. *(picks up the folder and reads)* "What's most curious about the patient is her total lack of concern regarding her condition. Her spirits are consistently good and she exhibits absolutely no anxiety about the future."

DANNY. Can it be because there is no future?

OLEANDER. *(lightly)* So, hey, why don't you just meet her?

DANNY. *(just as lightly)* So, hey, no.

OLEANDER. Well, you'll want to talk to her at least. Here's her chart, here's a tape recorder…

DANNY. No, I don't want to talk to her at least. Get off it, Ollie. Quit trying to seduce me.

OLEANDER. Surely you can spare a few days.

DANNY. Surely I can't.

OLEANDER. *(abruptly)* How long are you going to hang on to it, Danny?

DANNY. *(tightly)* I've forgotten it.

OLEANDER. Like hell you have! What is it, three years, four years?

DANNY. *(he turns to go)* See you around.

OLEANDER. God damn it, she needs you!

DANNY. Not me she doesn't.

OLEANDER. Then I need you!

DANNY. I'm not a working doctor. I'm on sabbatical. Sick leave. Time off. Furlough.

OLEANDER. You think it's easy for me? I'm having a hard time here!

DANNY. Not my problem.

OLEANDER. Listen Danny. They're breathing down my neck to get them in, turn them around, get them out. I can hold this patient for twenty-one days. Then she's lost to us. Someone we could study, someone we could learn from, someone we might even be able to help.

(Danny doesn't answer)

What's the big deal, Danny? Three lousy weeks.

DANNY. What am I supposed to do in three weeks?

OLEANDER. I don't know. And I don't have the time to stand here trying to convince you to do what you spent your goddam life learning how to do!

(And a pause)

Just meet her. I'd like your first impression.

(another pause)

Meet her. That's all I ask.

DANNY. All right, I'll meet her.

OLEANDER. Good.

DANNY. That's all.

OLEANDER. That's fine.

(Oleander puts his hand on Danny's shoulder)

And thanks.

DANNY. Now don't get maudlin on me.

(Lights up in Mary's room.)

MARY. *(at refrigerator)* Can I get you something to drink? What would you like?

ZELDA. Do you have caffein-free no-cal cola?

MARY. *(takes out a bottle)* How about club soda?

ZELDA. Is it sodium-free New York-style seltzer?

MARY. *(closing refrigerator door)* Look. This isn't going to be easy. Why don't you just go home?

ZELDA. Cele, Cele! Of course it will be easy. Just give yourself time! When I saw your picture in the paper, I didn't hesitate a minute! I said that is my old friend Cele and the minute she'll lay her eyes on me, it will all come rushing back to her! Now I'll admit, maybe it doesn't always work that way, you know, the way it does in movies, maybe it doesn't all come back in a rush – but at least something comes back, doesn't it?

MARY. I forgot your name.

ZELDA. *(losing patience)* Zelda!

MARY. Zelda! Zel-da! Zzzzzeee. Last letter of the alphabet. F. Scott Fitzgerald. Zelda! Got it.

ZELDA. Zelda Sterling and Cecilia Schooner. From the time we were in first grade we stood in line together, we had recess together, we got our periods together...

MARY. Cecilia Schooner?

ZELDA. We had our first dates together, we shaved our legs together, we let ourselves be felt up together...

MARY. *(holding up a hand to stop her)* Listen, Zelda, Why don't we call it a day, Zelda? There's a lot I have to absorb.

ZELDA. What are you absorbing? I haven't even told you any details.

MARY. Yes, yes, that's what I mean. I'm not ready for details. I have to take this a little at a time. Like right now I have to absorb that my name is Cecilia Schooner.

ZELDA. *(shaking her head in wonder)* Didn't you even know that?

MARY. No, I didn't. So I can't get into being felt up when I just learned what my name is. *(beat)* And what's your...

ZELDA. *(screaming)* ZELDA!

(Door opens as **OLEANDER** *enters,* **DANNY** *behind him.)*

ZELDA. *(continuing)* I don't believe this! She can't even remember my name!

OLEANDER. Thank you very much, Miss... ah... Miss... would you wait outside?

ZELDA. I don't believe this!

(Exits)

OLEANDER. Hello, Mary.

MARY. Hello.

OLEANDER. Do you remember me? I'm Doctor Oleander.

MARY. Of course I remember you. You're Doctor Oleander.

OLEANDER. I want you to meet a colleague of mine. Dr. Lucchesi...

DANNY. Danny.

OLEANDER. Yes. We were in med. school together.

(No one cares)

Actually, Doctor... Danny... is writing a book on amnesia.

MARY. Really?

DANNY. Yes. It's called "Amnesiacs I Have Known But Can't Quite Recall."

OLEANDER. Dr. Lucchesi...

DANNY. Danny.

OLEANDER. ...Danny is very interested in your case. So much, in fact, he's going to work with you and observe you and help you in every way he can.

DANNY. He means I've agreed to meet you.

OLEANDER. That's right.

DANNY. That's all.

MARY. That's fine.

OLEANDER. So I'll leave you now to get acquainted. If you need me, Doctor, you know where I am.

DANNY. Yes, Doctor. Thank you, Doctor.

(**OLEANDER** *sticks his clipboard into Danny's hand and leaves.* **DANNY** *slouches into a chair and opens a file folder.*)

I'd like to ask you some questions, Miss Smith.

MARY. Call me Mary.

DANNY. *(immediately alert)* Then you recognize Mary as your real name?

MARY. No. But I don't recognize Miss Smith, either. *(beat)* Zelda says my real name is Cecilia Kohler. Is it?

DANNY. Not Kohler. Schooner is what she said. We've got to check that out. In the meantime, the chart lists you as Mary Smith. Do you live in Chicago, Miss Smith?

MARY. Chicago? *(thinks)* Yes. What's with the names?

DANNY. *(looks up)* Pardon?

MARY. Why are you so carefully "Danny" and I, "Miss Smith"?

DANNY. *(smiles at this perception)* Bothers me. The doctor thing. Patient walks into a doctor's office and it's Doctor "So and So." But no matter how old or young the patient is, it's always the condescending first name.

MARY. And you don't do that with your patients.

DANNY. I don't have patients.

MARY. But you're a doctor.

DANNY. I don't practice.

MARY. Ah, you've perfected it.

DANNY. Bad joke.

MARY. *(shrugs)* I've been sick.

DANNY. I don't work with people any more.

MARY. What do you work with?

DANNY. Computers. Research. Writing.

(reading the notes)

You were found in the Loop, walking back and forth through the cars of the El train. Back and forth, back and forth. At each station, you paused and looked out of the car. But then you remained in the train, to continue your walk back and forth through the cars. Do you recall any of this, Mary?

MARY. No.

DANNY. When the police asked you what you were looking
for, you said, "a hundred and sixty-eighth street."

MARY. That's probably where I live.

DANNY. There is no one hundred and sixty-eighth Street
station in Chicago.

MARY. Ah.

DANNY. But there is one in New York City.

MARY. Well! Talk about being on the wrong train!

DANNY. What about your meeting today? With your childhood friend? *(glancing at a sheet of paper)* Zelda.

MARY. Zelda. She's a flake. I don't know if she's from my
past or a room down the hall. She's furious with me
because I can't remember her. Listen, did you know
my name was Kohler?

DANNY. Schooner.

MARY. Schooner? Not Kohler?

NURSE'S VOICE. All right, Mrs. Kohler, open your eyes.

DANNY. What is it?

MARY. The nurse – she says I should open my eyes.

DANNY. Yes? What else? What else are you recalling?

MARY. Nothing. *(immediately forgetting it)* How does she
know my name?

DANNY. Who? The nurse?

MARY. No. You know.

DANNY. *(thinks hard)* Zelda. *(refers to notes)* Okay. The report
says when the story broke about finding you in the "L,"
there were several responses. Some people thought
they recognized you. Some people just wanted to recognize you. Zelda's was the only story that made some
sense. She's originally from New York, she says, and
lives in Chicago now.

MARY. *(mildly curious)* Who were the others?

DANNY. Mostly families looking for long-lost daughters or wives or mothers.

MARY. How did you weed them out?

DANNY. Details didn't check. Some were foreign. Obviously, you're an American.

MARY. And a New Yorker.

DANNY. Ah! You remember that?

MARY. You told me.

DANNY. Oh.

MARY. Forget?

DANNY. I'm allowed to forget.

MARY. My, you're touchy. Listen, why don't you go home now?

DANNY. Do you remember anything?

MARY. No.

DANNY. Nothing?

MARY. Nothing.

MOTHER'S VOICE. Cele… help me out… don't leave me here…

MARY. *(winces)* Ah…

MOTHER'S VOICE. Don't let them keep me…

DANNY. *(immediately observant)* What is it?

MARY. *(pause. SHE turns to him)* I don't know. It's gone.

DANNY. But you remembered again, didn't you? You see, you do have memories. You are remembering some things.

MARY. It's like a tiny bird. Comes whizzing into my head. Whizzes right out.

DANNY. Yes? Does that happen often?

MARY. Now how would I know?

DANNY. Okay. The memory is a strange animal. It doesn't have good defenses. Almost anything can sit on it. Fear. Pride. Guilt. Always guilt. Always something negative. Everybody suffers memory lapses. Where did I put those keys? Next: Why did I lose them? Next: What's wrong with me? Finally: I'm no good. All these negative thoughts crowd into our brain – short-circuiting the one single solitary connection we need – where we put those keys!

(Mary gets into bed, pulls the covers over her head, finished with him)

And for my next intriguing lecture…

(walks to head of bed, peers down)

All right. Take it easy, read a book, watch TV, let it happen.

(starts to leave)

Don't be discouraged.

MARY. Oh, no, I'm not discouraged. Look how much we've accomplished already. I met Zelda. I found out my name is Mary Kohler. I learned I lived in Riverdale. That's an incredible lot in such a short time, isn't it?

DANNY. Riverdale?

MARY. You told me.

DANNY. I said New York. And it's not Mary, it's Cecilia.

MARY. Oh, yes.

DANNY. And not Kohler. Schooner.

MARY. Schooner? Yes, yes, that's right. It's not… what did I say… ?

DANNY. Kohler.

NURSE'S VOICE. Okay, Mrs. Kohler, open your eyes. It's all over.

MARY. All over?

DANNY. What is it? What are you remembering?

NURSE'S VOICE. It's all over. You can go home now.

MARY. The nurse said it's all over. I can go home now.

DANNY. Why would she say that?

NURSE'S VOICE. You'll have some cramping for a while. Then you'll be fine. The doctor did quite a bit of scraping.

MARY. Cramping? Scraping… ?

DANNY. An abortion?

> *(She doesn't answer)*

> Can you tell me when you had that abortion? Were you married?

MARY. Married?

MOTHER. Everybody gets married. That's how life is.

> *(Mary's **MOTHER** comes into the room. It is as though she is coming out of the wall. She is probably in her sixties now, though in her fifties and seventies at other times. Usually wears bright, cheerful colors – pinks, blues, yellows. A strong, honest woman.)*

MARY. *(to **DANNY**)* What difference does that make, if I'm married or not?

DANNY. If you were married, you had a husband. If we found your husband, we'd learn more about you.

MARY. In other words, I didn't exist until I was married.

DANNY. I didn't say that. But what is Kohler? Is that your married name?

MOTHER. Everybody gets married. Marriage makes the world go round.

MARY. *(turning to her)* Are you starting that again?

MOTHER. A girl like you should be married twelve times already.

MARY. Okay, I promise. This year I'm definitely getting married.

MOTHER. Get married and get divorced.

MARY. That's my plan.

MOTHER. That would make me happy.

MARY. That's also my plan, to make you happy. I want to make you proud. I want to please you. I want to please everybody!

MOTHER. Life is too long to be lived alone.

MARY. Yesterday you told me life is too short.

MOTHER. Life is too short to hold a grudge.

MARY. Where do you get these quotes? Do you have a little book hidden behind the refrigerator? "Mom's Merry Momisms?"

MOTHER. Don't wait for another Noel.

MARY. Noel? I've already forgotten him.

MOTHER. You don't want to end up alone and lonely.

MARY. You mean like you?

MOTHER. Me? Who says I'm alone?

MARY. What about Daddy? Where was he? Why wasn't he here?

MOTHER. Never mind that.

MARY. But the point is, now you're alone.

MOTHER. I'm not alone. I have you.

(**MOTHER** *walks out*)

DANNY. Who is Noel?

MARY. Noel?

DANNY. You mentioned him.

MARY. Did I?

DANNY. Just now. When you were telling me about your mother. Can you tell me who Noel is?

MARY. No.

DANNY. And what about Daddy?

MARY. Daddy?

DANNY. Yes, your father. Do you know…

MARY. *(shortly)* No! I don't know anything.

DANNY. Well, surely something is in your…

MARY. *(turning on him sharply)* Look, do me a favor! Go away. I'm not interested. Okay? I'm really not interested!

DANNY. How do you like it here? Are you comfortable in this room?

MARY. It's all right.

DANNY. Does anything in it look familiar? Any object? The chair? The sink? The walls?

MARY. The walls?

DANNY. *(instantly)* Yes? What about the walls?

(**NOEL** *enters, carrying a can of paint and a brush.*
NOEL *is about seventeen*)

NOEL. Just needs some paint. I love fresh paint.

MARY. Paint?

DANNY. Paint?

NOEL. I'll tell you my secret if you tell me yours.

(**MARY** *stiffens.* **NOEL** *leaves.*)

DANNY. What is it?

MARY. Oh, it's a secret.

DANNY. A secret? Well, can you…

MARY. No, I can't. If I did, it wouldn't be a secret, would
it?

(**DANNY** *waits another moment. Then, decides to move
on*)

DANNY. Okay. Let me show you something.

(*shows her the tape recorder*)

Are you familiar with this?

MARY. A tape recorder. You want me to talk into that when
I remember something?

DANNY. Anything. A color, a smell, a sound. This is the
record button. Just tape whatever you can remember. You may have a recollection – a dream… even a
secret.

MARY. (*punching in the button*) Hi. I'm not in to answer your
call right now…

DANNY. Ah. You had an answering machine.

MARY. "…thank you for calling and please talk right after
the beep." Beep.

(*clicks it off. Then, mouthing the words as* **MOTHER**
speaks)

MOTHER'S VOICE. (*imperiously*) Tell her her mother called!

MARY. I think she thought she was talking to my butler.

DANNY. You seem to remember your mother fairly well.

MARY. She was a woman of broad strokes. Brown eyes. Big ears. Her ears weren't always big. Just when she got old. *(pause)* I heard that ears never stop growing. She shrank. Oh, we women don't have it easy. We have our menstrual cramps and then we have our morning sickness and then our childbirth agonies and then we have our hot flashes and finally we shrink. But the ears go right on growing – just keep on growing along.

MOTHER. *(entering)* Tell her her mother called!

(comes into kitchen, takes off her apron)

DANNY. What was she like?

MARY. A mother. Just like all mothers. They get on your nerves when they're around. And when they're gone, you don't know how you're going to get through without them.

MOTHER. *(calling loudly)* I'm going to work. I left your lunch on the stove.

MARY. *(also loudly)* I'm going to work, too.

MOTHER. Before you go to work you should get a job.

MARY. Now who told you I lost my job?

MOTHER. Nobody has to tell me. You think I don't know my own daughter. What happened this time? Why did you lose your job?

MARY. The usual reason.

MOTHER. Ah! The boss was trying to get fresh with you! Those lousy men! Is he married?

MARY. I lost my job because it was boring. And I didn't do it well. And the pay was lousy. And yes, he's married. But don't worry. I have an interview Wednesday. Bergdorf. They're looking for a buyer.

MOTHER. You'll get it. You're the best there is!

(exits)

DANNY. What else?

MARY. She came from Vienna. Wien. She was confused about "v"s and "w"s. At election time, she would say "Ve must all wote."

DANNY. How does it make you feel when you think of her? Happy? Sad?

MARY. I don't think of her.

NOEL'S VOICE. Everybody out. I'm going to paint this room.

DANNY. Then nothing comes to mind.

MARY. Sometimes I remember odd things. Tiny little details.

DANNY. Good! What?

MARY. The tablecloth.

DANNY. Tablecloth?

MARY. It was plastic. And it had lots of little coffee pots and coffee cups and saucers all over it. Cheerful. Coffee is cheerful, don't you think?

DANNY. Do you know how to make coffee?

MARY. No.

MOTHER. *(entering, holding a cup of coffee)* What's to make? You put in some water, you put in some coffee, you put it on the stove. That's all.

   (sits at table)

MARY. I don't know how you do it, but you make the world's best coffee.

   (pouring coffee for them)

   How do you do it?

MOTHER. How do I do it? I do it.

MARY. *(joining her mother at the table)* That's how she was about her recipes. Once I called her to get her recipe for pot roast. I said, "Mother, how do you make a pot roast?" And she said, "Like anything else."

MOTHER. Like anything else.

   (sips her coffee and hums)

   Ah, nothing like a good cup of coffee.

MARY. That's right, Mom. That's entirely right. Say what you will about booze, sex and a fine cigar, there's nothing like a good cup of coffee!

(Mother is humming)

You like that song, don't you?

MOTHER. When I met your father – we met at a dance – our first dance was to that song. So it was "our song." Then he went to war. Came back four years later, a different person. We married anyway. At our wedding, we danced to that song. By then, he could hardly hear. The guns and the bombs had dulled his ears. What is that they say? The army makes a man out of you? It made a broken man out of him.

(sips coffee with pleasure)

Ah, nothing like a good cup of coffee!

(turning to Mary)

You remember your cousin Benjy moved to Florida?

MARY. Benjy? Yes. So?

MOTHER. He's getting married again.

MARY. Benjy? But I thought Benjy was impotent.

MOTHER. So? He has a car, doesn't he?

> (**MOTHER** *sips her coffee.* **MARY** *looks at her for a moment – then decides not to let this one pass unchallenged.*)

MARY. Mom, what has a car got to do with Benjy's impotence?

MOTHER. What's the matter with you? You need a car in Florida!

NOEL. *(entering, carrying his can of paint and a small ladder.)*
Okay, everybody out. I'm going to paint this room.

MOTHER. He's here again with the paint.

NOEL. This room looks dingy. I'll put on a coat of paint. It'll look nice and new and clean.

(starts painting)

I love fresh paint. Don't you love the smell of fresh paint?

MOTHER. *(turns again to **MARY**)* What is he wasting his time for?

NOEL. I get the paint from my father's place. You'll see what a difference a coat of paint makes.

MARY. My mother says it's too bad I didn't meet a boy whose father owns a jewelry store.

MOTHER. *(to* **MARY***)* Or a butcher.

NOEL. My father makes more money than a butcher. Much more money. Much much more more money.

MOTHER. So what? He's going to eat a can of paint for supper? You know what a steak costs today? or a brisket?

NOEL. I'm not saying a brisket isn't important…

MOTHER. Important? Nothing is more important than a brisket!

NOEL. I'm going to remember that.

MOTHER. Food is what makes the world go around!

> *(pats him on the cheek)*

> You're a good boy, Noel. Your heart's in the right place.

> *(***SHE*** leaves)*

NOEL. That's the most positive thing she's ever said to me.

MARY. My mother loves you. She knows you're going to save me from the horrors of a single life.

NOEL. But every time I come here, she gives me a dirty look.

MARY. That's not a dirty look, Noel. That's how she looks.

NOEL. *(sitting on the couch)* You want to sit on the couch with me?

MARY. My mother thinks we're too young.

NOEL. Too young for what?

MARY. Too young for what's popping up in your head.

NOEL. It's not my head it's popping up in.

> *(***SHE*** sits next to him on the couch. ***HE*** moves away)*

> But I'm always afraid I won't be able to control myself.

MARY. So? I'm not afraid. Aren't you curious?

NOEL. Sure I am, you know I am. It's all I can do to keep from doing it. Sometimes I think I'll pass out if I don't. But Cissy – if we do – what if you get pregnant?

MARY. Then we'll have a baby. It's about time I had a baby.

NOEL. What? But we're not even finished with high school! And we have to go to college! Maybe graduate school! Who knows? What would we do for money?

MARY. Your father's rich. Why do you think I go with you?

NOEL. But I don't want him to support our baby! God! We'd never heard the end of it. And neither would the baby. Can you imagine when the baby is grown up and my father is telling him "when you were a baby I bought you diapers and I paid for your first tricycle and..."

MARY. *(covering her ears)* Oh, stop! I can't bear it! You're worrying about what your father's going to tell our baby when he's grown up and I'm still a virgin!

NOEL. *(morosely)* I know. It's a terrible habit. I do it all the time. I wake up and while I'm in bed, I'm thinking, well, I'll get up and take a pee and then I'll brush my teeth and comb my hair and today I'll wear my argyle socks and my green sweater. And I get up and it's like I'm doing it all for the second time! *(distressed)* And when I'm walking home from school, I think, well, after this block, I'll walk up Holland Avenue and then I'll cut through the lots and cross over by the drug store... *(yelling)* And it makes the walk twice as long! I walk once in my head and once on my feet! It's exhausting!

MARY. *(sympathetically)* Maybe you'll grow out of it.

NOEL. It's a curse.

(kneeling down next to her)

I love you, Cissy.

MARY. *(throwing her arms around him)* I love you, too.

NOEL. I love you more every day. I love you so much. I'm giving you all my love. I'm not holding anything back. I could never love anyone the way I love you.

KRU. *(appearing)* You told me you love to walk.

(**LIZ KRUGER** *is at this point in her mid-twenties, a put-together good-looking woman who takes good care of herself. She is in excellent shape – if not a runner, certainly someone who believes in exercise. She has a strong positive attitude, an easy smile, an easy manner. She wears good clothes, tailored, sporty, expensive.*)

MARY. (*turning to her*) I did?

KRU. It's the only way to see Europe.

NOEL. We have it all ahead of us, Cissy. We'll get married and have babies and have our own home and we'll be together all the time. It's all ahead of us. Everything to look forward to…

(**NOEL** *disappears.* **KRU** *remains.*)

(*Lights remain up in Mary's room. Lights go up in doctor's area. Oleander stands watching. Danny joins him*)

OLEANDER. Who is she?

DANNY. I don't know. Mary can describe what she looks like. That's fairly clear. But she can't tell me her name. Who she is.

OLEANDER. Can't? Or won't?

DANNY. No idea. She's obviously fearful of remembering her. Yet – she doesn't want to let her go.

OLEANDER. Can you keep her in that memory?

DANNY. No. They come and go and I don't know what the pattern is.

OLEANDER. You will.

(*Danny turns and gives him a good hard look*)

OLEANDER. (*continuing; shrugs*) Three lousy weeks.

(*He walks off. Danny picks up some CDs and returns to Mary's room.* **KRU** *is still there*)

DANNY. I brought you some music. Abbey Road… Madonna… Glenn Miller… some Bach, Mozart…

MARY. You expect me to listen to all that? You think I have nothing else to do with my time?

DANNY. Just play them as background. Sometimes music can recall an incident. How's it going?

MARY. Oh, fine, fine. Everything's beginning to fall into place.

(walks around the room, glancing at KRU *who sits on the bench near the bed)*

The memories are just clicking along. A door opening. A light at the end of the tunnel. I hear music, the faint strains of an almost-familiar tune.

DANNY. I'm sorry I asked.

KRU. She's very gifted. She has a natural talent.

MARY. Well, listen… my mind is not a total blank.

DANNY. I know your mind is not a total blank. The memories are there, stuffed in a file cabinet. Trouble is you can't get that file drawer open. Sometimes it opens a crack – you remember – and then it slams shut. That's why you can't sustain the memory.

MARY. So there we are. Might as well call the whole thing off.

DANNY. But I'll do that. I'll collect them for you and put them in my file cabinet. Then maybe I can help you sort them out and maybe put one or two or four or six in perspective so you can have a complete memory that can help us.

MARY. Such as?

DANNY. Such as who you are.

KRU. Don't you want to stay? There's plenty of room.

MARY. *(turning to her)* How can I? It's impossible!

KRU. Anything else is impossible.

DANNY. *(softly prompting her)* What's impossible?

MARY. *(turns to him)* What? What are you talking about?

DANNY. *(her agitation is increasing – he moves on)* Memories are dependent on your mood. We tend to recall happy moments when we're happy, sad times when we're depressed.

MARY. *(Continuing to walk around the room, somewhat aimlessly)* Yes, that makes sense.

TAMMY'S VOICE. She was my friend. Now she's yours.

MARY. She's our friend!

TAMMY'S VOICE. Bullshit.

KRU. There are other ways to be happy.

> *(And she exits)*

MOTHER. *(entering, by the couch)* Cele... help me out... don't let them keep me...

> *(and walks off)*

DANNY. Keep her where?

MARY. I don't know. I can't remember.

DANNY. *(aware of her increasing anxiety)* You are remembering. Don't stop it, let it happen!

MARY. Nothing makes sense.

> *(**MARY** starts to pace)*

DANNY. *(watching her closely)* That's all right. What we're doing here is like dominoes. One memory kicks off another... and another.

MARY. Sure, right.

DANNY. *(trying to keep her on track)* Not necessarily in sequence. The mind doesn't remember chronologically.

MARY. Yes, absolutely. Okay.

> *(Her pacing is more frantic. Opens cupboard, closes it, opens the refrigerator, looks in, closes it.)*

DANNY. But we can match them up later...

MARY. *(almost hysterical)* Later! Later! Yes, later, we'll do it later! I have to go now!

DANNY. *(instantly)* Go? Where?

MARY. Yes, yes, I've got to get going.

> *(shakes his hand, walks to door.)*

It was nice meeting you. I'll see you in a little.

> *(reaches door, turns the knob. It is locked.)*

DANNY. Where do you want to go?

MARY. *(lightly, trying to cover the stress in her voice)* No place. No place special. Just for a walk.

DANNY. A walk?

MARY. *(wrestles with the doorknob)* Yes… I have to make a phone call…

DANNY. Here's a phone…

MARY. What the hell is wrong with this door?

DANNY. Why don't you make your call here?

MARY. Is this locked? Am I locked in?

(SHE is beginning to tremble)

DANNY. I'll dial it for you. What's the number?

MARY. *(shaking the door)* Let me out of here!

DANNY. Listen to me! There's a phone number in your head. You may not be aware of it, but it's there, it's in your head. Don't concentrate on it, just let it come to you…

MARY. *(turning to him)* Why don't you open this door for me, okay? I just have to take this little walk and make this call and I'll be back in a jiffy, no time at all…

DANNY. I wish I could, Mary, but it's much too soon…

MARY. *(SHE is now perspiring profusely – clearly SHE is having an anxiety attack)*

I got to get out! You have no right to lock me up!

DANNY. Who do you want to call, Mary? Your mother?

MARY. *(startled)* What?

DANNY. Your mother? Your mom? Your mommy?

MARY. Mommy?

TAMMY. *(off)* Mommy!

MARY. What?

DANNY. Is that who you want to call, Mary?

MARY. *(turning to him)* Who?

TAMMY. *(offstage)* Mommy! Mommy!

MARY. Yes?

TAMMY. Mommy, they gave me cookies to sell!

(**TAMMY** *enters, wearing a Girl Scout uniform and carrying several boxes of cookies. Here,* **TAMMY** *is about eleven.* **SHE** *is a darling girl, shy, quiet, polite, but not cloying, bright enough to take care of herself without being arrogant about it*)

MARY. Cookies?

TAMMY. They cost a dollar. All the Girl Scouts are selling them. Will you buy a box, Mom?

MARY. (*turning to* **DANNY**) Mom? I have a daughter?

DANNY. I don't know. Do you?

MARY. I don't know. I always wanted children.

DANNY. Do you?

MARY. A daughter? I can't remember.

DANNY. Maybe you will.

MARY. I don't think so. There's nothing in my head. Nothing.

DANNY. What's your daughter's name?

MARY. Tammy.

TAMMY. What?

MARY. (*looks at* **DANNY** *and smiles. Then turns to* **TAMMY**) Tammy, how many boxes have you sold?

TAMMY. None. And I've been selling them all day! Will you buy a box?

MARY. Me? But Tammy, that's like selling it to yourself.

TAMMY. If you buy a box, Mom, at least I'll have sold one.

MARY. That's not quite cricket, is it?

TAMMY. (*forlornly, nearly tremulous*) If you don't, I'll be the only Scout who didn't sell even one single box!

MARY. (*turning in pain to* **DANNY**) Oh, God! Did I buy it? Did I buy it?

(**TAMMY** *leaves*)

DANNY. Think. Think about it! What else do you remember?

MARY. (*the memory is gone*) What else?

DANNY. You have a daughter. How old is she? Where is she?

MARY. Yes. I have a daughter. Where is she? How old is she? She may need me. I've got to find her.

(*But she turns to the bed*)

I think I'll take a little nap.

DANNY. But what about her? What about Tammy?

MARY. As a rule, I don't like afternoon naps. It throws off my metabolism. Or my karma. Or something. I wake up and every fiber in my body is standing up and screaming like a headfull of uncombed hair.

DANNY. But you're going to take a nap now?

MARY. Certainly not, how can I with this screaming hair? But I'm tired. I didn't sleep well last night. (*beat*) Or was it the night before?

DANNY. Did you dream?

MARY. I think so.

DANNY. Do you remember what you dreamed?

MARY. Are you kidding?

DANNY. Lost my head.

(*He walks out into doctor's area.* **ZELDA** *joins him*)

DANNY. (*continuing*) What do you know about a daughter?

ZELDA. Nothing.

DANNY. Nothing?

ZELDA. We lost touch after high school. I heard she had a good job.

DANNY. Doing what?

ZELDA. I don't know. Merchandising. Marketing. Something with an M.

DANNY. Buyer?

ZELDA. That's it.

DANNY. What about Noel?

ZELDA. He was really cute. He was her only boyfriend. She never dated anyone else.

DANNY. How do you know? You stopped talking when you were eighteen.

ZELDA. Well. I heard.

DANNY. She said something about a secret.

ZELDA. Everybody has secrets.

DANNY. Do you?

ZELDA. Don't you?

DANNY. Does she?

ZELDA. Maybe.

DANNY. Maybe?

(**ZELDA** *gives a noncommittal shrug*)

Maybe you can bring it up in the conversation.

ZELDA. Leave it to me.

DANNY. Gently.

ZELDA. Of course gently.

(*Lights up in Mary's room as Zelda walks in*)

ZELDA. (*continuing; She hands her a book*) Here. I brought you a book to read.

MARY. I have a book. It's around here someplace, I'll show it to you…

ZELDA. A book? How long can you read one book?

MARY. Me? Forever. By the time I get to the end of the book, I've forgotten the beginning and I can start all over again. It's wonderful. And cheap.

ZELDA. (*taking a paper bag out of her purse*) Would you rather have chocolate nut cookies? I brought these for you, too.

MARY. No, thanks.

ZELDA. (*starting to eat one*) I read in an etiquette book that the gift you give should be the gift you like to receive.

MARY. Now you can see why.

ZELDA. Of course, I never eat them anymore. I hate to tell you how fattening they are. Not that you should worry. You never had a weight problem. I never did either until I was thirty. Then everything I ate turned to fat.

Cottage cheese. Lean fish. Name it. So what's this
about a secret?

MARY. I don't know.

ZELDA. Kids are big on secrets. We all had secrets. I had
one, too. *(beat)* Do you remember what mine was?

MARY. Your what?

ZELDA. My secret.

(Mary doesn't answer)

You don't know?

(Mary just sighs)

Okay. My secret was that I was bow-legged.

MARY. Some big deal secret.

ZELDA. It was to me! I was very self-conscious about it!

MARY. Maybe, but it was no secret. Anybody who looked at
your legs knew your secret.

ZELDA. Look, Cele, I didn't come here to be insulted.

MARY. Then why do you come? Why don't you just stay
home, reading a good book and eating chocolate nut
cookies?

ZELDA. Your doctor seems to feel I'm important! He's asked
me to come back. But maybe I won't. And maybe you'll
be sorry.

MARY. Yes, I'm sorry. I'm sorry I don't like your cookies.
I'm sorry you're bow-legged.

NOEL. *(entering)* Okay. I've got a secret.

MARY. *(turning to him)* Secret? What is it?

NOEL. It's a real secret.

ZELDA. You thought if you dated Noel, you could get away
with anything!

MARY. What the hell does that mean?

(Zelda exits)

NOEL. I'll tell you my secret if you tell me yours.

MARY. *(turning to him)* That sounds like I'll show you my
thing if you show me yours.

NOEL. Okay, I'll show you my thing if you show me yours.

MARY. You tell me your secret first.

NOEL. Right. *(silence – then he giggles nervously)* It's hard. I mean, it's harder than I thought to tell you.

MARY. Oh. Well. That's okay, Noel. You don't have to tell me.

NOEL. No. I want to. (**HE** *starting to perspire.*) I want you to know. I'll tell you. It's just… *(giggles)* This is hard.

MARY. All right, I'll go first.

NOEL. You will?

MARY. Sure. This is a secret nobody else in the world knows. Except my mother. And me. And now you. *(staring straight ahead)* My secret is about my father.

MOTHER. *(enters, stands off on the side)* Don't tell anyone.

MARY. *(having gotten that much out, **SHE** takes a short breath – and barges ahead)*

I think he's in a mental hospital.

MOTHER. Nobody has to know where he is or why.

MARY. I'm pretty sure of it. Way out in Long Island. I think it's called Pilgrim State Hospital. I think it's in Patchogue. That's all the way in…

NOEL. I know where it is. *(softly)* You don't have to tell me anymore.

MARY. I don't know anymore to tell you.

MOTHER. *(exiting)* It will only go against you.

NOEL. God. That's a real secret.

MARY. You won't tell anyone?

NOEL. It will die with me, Cissy. I promise.

(puts his arms around her)

I'm glad you told me.

MARY. Why?

NOEL. It makes me feel closer to you. I know something nobody else knows. That's special. *(pause)* I don't have that kind of secret to tell you. But – what the hell.

MARY. You don't have to tell me.

NOEL. A deal is a deal. *(takes a breath)* My secret is when I'm with you… when I go home… I get so hot… with you… when we stand… close to each other… rub against each other… ah… I…

MARY. I know.

NOEL. When I go home… my sh… shorts are wet.

MARY. *(doesn't quite know what to do with that)* Well.

> *(turns to him with a big smile)*

Thanks for telling me.

NOEL. That's not the secret.

> *(she waits patiently)*

I don't want my mother to see, you know, when she does the laundry. So… ah… so I throw them out.

MARY. You throw them out? Your shorts?

NOEL. Yep. Buy a new pair. Half my allowance goes for underwear.

MARY. Jesus! What a secret!

> *(**SHE** starts to laugh. **NOEL** laughs with her)*

MOTHER. *(entering)* What is with you and that boy? All you do is laugh.

> *(Noel walks out)*

MARY. That's not all we do.

MOTHER. I don't want to know about it.

MARY. Listen, we were talking about Daddy.

MOTHER. Don't tell anybody about your father.

MARY. What's the big secret?

MOTHER. It's not a secret. If anybody asks you, you don't have to answer. Just say you don't know.

MARY. I don't know.

MOTHER. Fine. Keep it that way.

MARY. Why won't you tell me about him?

MOTHER. I just told you.

> *(She exits)*

DANNY. But she didn't tell you.

MARY. I was just a kid. Not terribly assertive.

DANNY. Did you get more assertive as you got older?

MARY. Oh, ho ho ho. When my mother was dying, they stuck a respirator down her throat. Without asking or anything, just stuck it down into her throat. She hated it, she tried to pull it out, but they tied her hands to the bed. I went to the doctor and I said, listen you doctor, I want you to take that tube out of her. He said no. I said, but I'm her daughter and I want that tube out! And he said, then you pull it out. And walked away.

(looking at **DANNY***)*

And walked away.

DANNY. You can't just take a patient off a respirator. The patient has to be weaned off and it takes a day or…

MARY. *(viciously)* Oh, shut up! Don't you understand? She was in a coma! An irreversible coma!

DANNY. Nothing is irreversible.

TAMMY. *(appearing)* Why did you put her in the hospital?

MARY. What else could I do? She's too sick to stay home.

TAMMY. She's going to die there.

MARY. *(turning to* **DANNY***)* What could I do? You don't put someone in the hospital to die! You put them there to get better!

DANNY. Did she get better?

MARY. Better? No, I think she died.

DANNY. You think?

MARY. Or maybe I dreamed it. Mothers don't die, do they? They don't get sick and they don't run away. They just get annoyed.

TAMMY. Why did you put her in the hospital?

MARY. God damn it, it wasn't my decision. The doctors know best!

TAMMY. You're her daughter! It's your decision!

DANNY. Why was she so angry with you?

MARY. Well, well, what do you expect? Tammy's young. She loves her grandmother – she doesn't want her to be sick. Nobody wants her to be sick!

DANNY. Why are you getting agitated?

MARY. Oh, get off it! Don't make a big deal out of everything! Tammy and I are very close. I was close to my mother too. I just couldn't confide in her.

TAMMY. Why not?

MARY. I don't know. Some things I just couldn't tell her.

TAMMY. Like what? What? What can't you tell me?

(Mary doesn't answer. Tammy walks off)

DANNY. What couldn't you tell her?

MARY. Why do you keep asking me these questions? How do you expect me to remember? I have amnesia!

DANNY. It's not just amnesia. Do you know what fugue means?

MARY. Fugue? *(thinks)* Music. Johann Sebastian Bach. How's that?

DANNY. Okay, that's one definition. Two contrapuntal melodies merging and becoming one. The first melody is running away, the second melody is chasing it. It's actually from the Latin "fugae" – the act of running away.

MARY. So I have a case of running away? From what?

DANNY. Yes. From what. Fugue is a very rare form of amnesia. You are literally running away from an unspeakable act. An unbearable memory. Actually during the fugue "lapse", the patient... you... might perform acts of which you have no recollection.

MARY. You mean I might have killed someone? And not remember it?

DANNY. I doubt it. I don't think you have the killer in you.

MARY. No? Has anyone seen Zelda?

DANNY. What we need to find out is what made you start running in the first place?

MARY. What do you think it was?

DANNY. Something that happened. Something that might have happened. Or never happened. Something you were afraid of. Or ashamed of. Wiping it out is your unconscious attempt to escape any conflict.

MARY. But why don't I remember anything?

DANNY. But you do. You remember Tammy, don't you?

MARY. Tammy? My daughter.

DANNY. She was selling Girl Scout cookies.

MARY. Girl Scout?

TAMMY. *(in the distance)* Well, guess what?

DANNY. You want to remember Tammy, don't you?

TAMMY. Well, guess what?

MARY. Oh, yes! Tammy's a remarkable girl! Full of surprises!

TAMMY. *(walks on.* **SHE** *wears camp shorts and shirt)*
Well, guess what? I got this part in our camp play. "The Mikado."

MARY. You?

TAMMY. Yes. We have rehearsals every day after activities. The play goes on at the end of the summer.

MARY. But I never knew you were interested in acting.

TAMMY. I'm not. Everyone in the senior bunk had to audition. It's our final activity.

MARY. Oh, I see. You mean everyone has a part in the show.

TAMMY. Yes, that's right. Will you come up to see it? All the parents are invited.

MARY. Of course, I'll come up to see it, darling. I did "The Mikado", too, when I was in high school. I was in the chorus. You're in the chorus, right?

TAMMY. No. I'm the lead.

(She takes a step forward and in a very compelling voice, begins to sing)

ON A TREE BY A RIVER A LITTLE TOM TIT
SANG "WILLOW TIT WILLOW TIT WILLOW".

AND I SAID TO HIM, "DICKIE BIRD, WHY DO YOU SIT?
SINGING WILLOW, TIT WILLOW, TIT WILLOW?"

(As **MARY** *listens to* **TAMMY,** **SHE** *is at first nervous and
self-conscious. Then, because* **TAMMY** *is good,* **SHE** *is
delighted)*

"IS IT WEAKNESS OF INTELLECT, BIRDIE",I CRIED
OR A RATHER TOUGH WORM IN YOUR LITTLE
INSIDE?"
WITH A SHAKE OF HIS POOR LITTLE HEAD,
HE REPLIED: "OH, WILLOW, TIT WILLOW, TIT
WILLOW."

*(***KRU** *slowly walks out, wearing camp counselor outfit.
Stands listening, unnoticed by* **MARY**.*)*

HE SLAPPED AT HIS CHEST AS HE SAT ON THAT
BOUGH
SINGING "WILLOW, TIT WILLOW, TIT WILLOW."
AND A COLD PERSPIRATION BESPANGLED HIS BROW
"OH, WILLOW, TIT WILLOW, TIT WILLOW."
THEN HE SOBBED AND HE SHOOK AND A GURGLE
HE GAVE
AS HE PLUNGED HIMSELF INTO THE BILLOWY WAVE
AND AN ECHO AROSE FROM THE SUICIDE'S GRAVE:
"OH WILLOW, TIT WILLOW, TIT WILLOW."

MARY. *(applauding)* Tammy, you were good! You were so
good!

TAMMY. *(the quintessential teenager)* Oh, God, no, I was awful!
Weren't you embarrassed, Mom?

MARY. Not at all, Tammy! Okay, I'll be honest with you.
When you first started, I thought, oh, Lord, she doesn't
know how to sing! But you do, Tammy! What kind of
mother am I not to know that you can sing?

KRU. *(stepping forward)* Nobody knew, believe me. Tammy
never auditioned for any of our shows, not even our
little weekly skits…

TAMMY. Certainly not. I'm terrible!

KRU. But it's the job of the music counselor to get
every camper involved in our big production, the

end-of- summer extravaganza. Up steps Tammy, does
her little bit – and lo and behold, we have our Lord
High Executioner!

MARY. I think this is wonderful for Tammy. I really can't
believe she's actually doing this. She's very shy...

TAMMY. No, I'm not.

MARY. Yes, you are.

KRU. Tammy? Not at all! She's very popular – she has lots
of friends. Captain of the swim team. And now – our
musical star!

MARY. No wonder she's so happy here. She wrote me that I
must come up and see the grounds... and go canoeing
with her on the lake... and of course, I must meet Kru,
that's all she writes about, the fabulous Liz Kruger!
And to think, I was hesitant about sending her here. I
was afraid she'd be homesick...

KRU. Not a chance! Tammy's a very special girl. I wouldn't
be surprised if she made All-Around Camper. And I
guess the credit for that goes to you.

MARY. Oh? Really? Do you think so? *(smiles at her)* All right
then. I'll take it.

(sings)

AND IF YOU REMAIN CALLOUS AND OBDURATE, I
SHALL PERISH AS HE DID AND YOU SHALL KNOW
WHY

MARY & TAMMY.

THOUGH I PROBABLY SHALL NOT EXCLAIM AS I DIE
OH, WILLOW, TIT WILLOW TIT WILLOW

(Lights fade. Oleander enters with coffee and a coke.)

OLEANDER. The daughter may be a runaway. That or living
with her father. Mary's husband. But why hasn't he
come forward? We had a press conference, we put her
on television. Where is he?

(He glances at Danny. No answer)

Maybe he's dead. Or married. Or living in Europe. Or
Asia.

DANNY. Or Mars.

OLEANDER. Or there is no father.

DANNY. Get me off this, Ollie.

OLEANDER. Why?

DANNY. It's too much for me. I'm panicking.

OLEANDER. You're doing fine. She likes you. She trusts you.

DANNY. Why should she? I'm bringing her closer to whatever it is she doesn't want to remember. And when she gets close, she gets uncomfortable. So do I!

OLEANDER. You're making headway.

DANNY. Like I was making headway the last time.

OLEANDER. Forget Belzer!

DANNY. Oh, how nice. How simple. Forget.

OLEANDER. That's right! Move on! Christ, Danny, it breaks my heart! You're sitting on park benches feeding pigeons when you should be here!

DANNY. Ah, is that it, Doctor Oleander? I was wondering why I was the lucky guy to get this job when you have an entire staff of qualified full-time psychiatrists.

OLEANDER. Because you're different. You think weird. What did you say to Mary about an irreversible coma? Nothing is irreversible. You really believe that?

DANNY. Yes, I do.

OLEANDER. And remember when we were in school and the Attending said this patient is terminal? Remember what you said? "Terminal is where they put trains." *(chuckling)* Trains…

DANNY. That isn't why you got me here, Ollie. I know the tricks. Get him out, get him working, he'll come out of it, he'll recover.

OLEANDER. So what's wrong with that?

DANNY. Maybe I won't recover. Maybe I'll get worse. Maybe I'll die.

OLEANDER. You won't get worse. In time, it'll be easy.

DANNY. Easy? Mary Smith has it easy. No memory. No waking up in the dead of night, soaking wet, screaming head, what did I do, what did I do, how could I do that!

OLEANDER. How the hell do you know she doesn't wake in the dead of night? Or the dead of day? And start running!

DANNY. It's no good, Ollie. It's not working.

OLEANDER. But it is! She is remembering!

DANNY. It's not working for me! I worry. I worry all the time. Every question I ask, I worry, is it the right one, am I going too fast, will I set her off, make it worse? Am I going to fuck up?

OLEANDER. Again? Is that what you mean?

(Startled, Danny looks at him)

You didn't play by the rules with Phillip Belzer.

DANNY. Oh, fuck the rules! This what-are-you-thinking, don't reveal, don't touch, don't hug is bullshit! Why can't we hug? An untouched infant dies!

OLEANDER. You brought him home. You brought your patient to your home!

DANNY. He was schizoid, panphobic. He felt completely isolated. He needed to belong! He needed a friend!

OLEANDER. You're not a friend! You're not Danny! To me, you're Danny, to your mother, to your chums, you're Danny! To your patient, you're Doctor Lucchesi!

DANNY. He was getting better. He went out. He rode the subway, he talked to people, he got a job. He was better. He really was.

OLEANDER. *(quietly)* Yes. He was better.

DANNY. Yes, he was better.

(He sits, thoroughly dejected)

OLEANDER. *(concerned)* Danny…

DANNY. But not enough. I misjudged. I didn't give him enough time.

OLEANDER. All right. So you misjudged. You think you're the only one? *(beat)* Bad things happen, Danny. And they pass and go away or we learn to live with them. You have another patient now. She needs help. She needs your help.

DANNY. How can I help her? I'm just as lost as she is.

OLEANDER. Danny, she's remembering Kru. Who is Kru? What happened to Tammy? Is she dead? Was Mary Smith in some way responsible for her disappearance? Did she kill her?

DANNY. You want me to help her remember that?

OLEANDER. You bet.

DANNY. *(slight pause)* Well. The least I can do is get her well and put her back in the work force so she can pay me.

(**HE** *smiles.* **OLEANDER** *doesn't*)

When treating an amnesiac, it's wise to collect your fee in advance.

OLEANDER. Do me a favor, Danny. Just stay objective. I worry about you.

DANNY. I worry about you, too. You never laugh at my jokes.

OLEANDER. Jokes?

DANNY. *(walking away)* Never mind.

(*Lights up in* **MARY**'s *room.* **DANNY** *walks in, hands her a gift box.*)

DANNY. *(continuing)* I brought you a gift.

MARY. Please, God, no chocolate-nut cookies.

DANNY. Open it.

MARY. This could lead to all kinds of complications. What would your wife say?

DANNY. My wife?

MARY. Aha! Caught you! A married man, eh?

DANNY. I never said that.

MARY. No, you didn't. That was a trick question anyway. I knew you weren't married. I could spot it the minute you walked in here. You have lots of women. But you are definitely not married.

DANNY. But I am.

MARY. I knew it! What's she like?

DANNY. You know we're not here to talk about me.

MARY. Just tell me where you met her.

DANNY. I met her in high school.

MARY. Then you got married and went to college together?

DANNY. I went to college. She went to work.

MARY. So you could go to college.

DANNY. That's right. Open your gift.

MARY. Now what will she say when she hears that you're showering me with gifts obviously of a highly personal and intimate nature…

(opens gift)

…how lovely! A jogging suit. I'll treasure it forever.

DANNY. *(taking articles out of a bag)* And here are socks, shoes and a pedometer. Now when you have this overwhelming urge to run, you can do it right here on the track in back of the clinic. It's healthy – and you won't get lost!

MARY. Well, that's a very nice gift, Dan. I thank you. But I'm still locked up! You're just letting me out in the yard with the other cons.

DANNY. Okay. How about lunch? Would you like to go out for lunch today?

MARY. Lunch?

NOEL. *(walking on, in shorts and tee shirt, carrying a beach towel)*

Just don't do tunafish.

MARY. Why, yes, that would be very nice. Where shall I meet you?

DANNY. I'll pick you up.

MARY. Oh, no, it's out of your way.

KRU. *(enters)* Doesn't matter. I'll be picking you up at the airport.

MARY. *(turning to her)* But I'm coming in at rush hour, you'll get into that horrible traffic.

KRU. I don't mind. You can tell me all about your trip – we'll stop for a bite of dinner. I don't mind at all. I want to do it for you.

MARY. How sweet. How awfully sweet. What time?

DANNY. How about twelve?

(Kru exits)

MARY. Fine. I'll pack some sandwiches.

NOEL. Just don't do tunafish again. It leaks right through the wrapping. You making it with mayonnaise?

MARY. Well, sure. What's tunafish without mayonnaise? Just fishy fish.

NOEL. Mayonnaise goes bad in the sun. You can get botulism and die.

MARY. *(with a sigh)* Okay. No tunafish sandwiches. Do you know something, Noel? We spend most of our time talking about food. While we're eating lunch, we're talking about where to go for dinner.

NOEL. Yes, I know. I thought we'd have dinner on City Island. How do you feel about lobster?

MARY. It's nine o'clock in the morning. How *can* I feel about lobster?

NOEL. I was thinking – maybe we should elope.

MARY. Elope? What an old-fashioned word.

NOEL. How does it strike you?

MARY. It's like the "vapors". She took to her bed with the vapors.

NOEL. Cissy, I'm dead serious.

MARY. Why should we elope? Don't you want a nice wedding? With bridesmaids – flowers. Gifts. A catered dinner. Chicken... roast beef. We could spend months talking about the smorgasbord.

NOEL. It's got a little to do with my mother.

MARY. What about your mother?

NOEL. She's afraid we'll get married.

MARY. I see. So that's why you want to elope?

> (*Noel is silent in the face of this logic. Then…*)

NOEL. Maybe we can have ham and cheese on a French roll with Russian dressing…

KRU. (*walking on, carrying a wicker picnic basket*) Anybody can do sandwiches.

NOEL. (*his voice fading out as he exits*) …or a corned beef and pastrami combo on seeded rye…

> (**NOEL** *exits as* **TAMMY** *enters with Kru, carrying a badminton set.* **KRU** *unpacks the basket, spreads a cloth, takes out glasses, plates, French bread.*)

KRU. There's no reason why we can't have a cold chicken and brie and Chardonnay and linen napkins…

MARY. (*laughs, delighted, as* **SHE** *joins them*) No reason at all as long as you've brought it all!

KRU. (*taking out thermos*) …iced peppermint tea for Tammy.

TAMMY. Guess what else she has in that basket, Mom?

MARY. (*peering in*) A waiter?

KRU. Better than that.

> (*takes out cassette player*)

> A bit of Bach.

> (*And a Bach fugue begins*)

TAMMY. When you get to know Kru, Mom, you'll find she's never without music.

> (*listens*)

> Oh, Kru, I know that one! That's "The Well Tempered Klavier".

KRU. Very good, Tammy.

TAMMY. We heard it at Carnegie Hall last month. It was an

incredible concert! You ought to come with us next
time we go to a concert, Mom. And in two weeks, Kru's
taking me rock-climbing! Mom, would you like to…

MARY. Tammy, don't even ask. Why in the world would I
ever want to climb a rock?

TAMMY. Well, that's why I wanted you to get to know Kru.
You're much too sedentary , Mom. You need to get out
and do something in the fresh air!

MARY. *(to Kru)* I suppose that's why you look so exuberantly
healthy. You exercise or something, right?

KRU. Or something. I jog…

TAMMY. … and skate and ski and jump rope…

MARY. Stop, you're exhausting me!

TAMMY. And play badminton!

> *(grabbing the badminton)*

I'll set this up up for us.

> *(runs out)*

MARY. God, I'm going to miss her when she leaves for
college.

KRU. College? That's a few years off, isn't it?

MARY. Well, I thought I'd start worrying about it now. She
wants to live on campus. I wish I could have gone to an
out of town college. Live in a dorm, pledge a sorority.
How about you, Kru?

KRU. Actually, I went to school in Switzerland.

MARY. Can't get more out of town than that.

KRU. You know, we'd love to have her come back next
summer as a junior counselor.

MARY. I don't know. I'd like her to do something more productive than camp.

> *(stops, embarrassed)*

Oh, I don't mean that you're not productive – what I
mean is…

> *(There is a pause. They both know why)*

I mean, it's different for you, Kru. After all, you're a teacher. You have your summers off.

KRU. I'm not a teacher.

MARY. No? How odd. Now why did I think you were a teacher?

KRU. *(amused)* Probably because I have my summers off.

MARY. It's none of my business. But what do you do?

KRU. Actually, I'm studying for my master's in music history. Then I'll probably go for my doctorate.

MARY. A student. So that's why you have your summers off.

KRU. Well, I have my winters off, too. I don't really have to work.

MARY. *(turning to DANNY)* I should have guessed she was rich. Rich people look different than poor people. They have more hair. Their teeth are whiter.

(to Kru)

Their fillings don't show when they laugh. Why is that?

KRU. I'd like you to come to my place sometime. There's a pool on the roof of the building. They keep it toasty warm even in winter. You could swim to your heart's delight. I don't want to brag, but I'm a pretty good cook. We'll light a fire, crack a bottle of wine. *(beat)* It could be fun.

(MARY starts to move away)

DANNY. Go on. Keep going.

KRU. I have quite a good music library. Do you like opera?

DANNY. Yes? yes? What else?

KRU. Perhaps you could come next weekend. Friday? Saturday?

(MARY moves back into the room. The memory is gone.)

DANNY. Did you go that Friday? Did you go to Kru's?

MARY. Well. Well. *(thinks)* I don't know.

DANNY. Why did you stop, Mary? Why didn't you want to stay in that memory? Was it painful?

MARY. Painful? Oh, no. It's just that it's...

(and looks up, blankly. KRU *has packed up the wicker basket and exits)*

It's gone.

DANNY. What about Kru? Did Tammy go rock-climbing with her? Mary, what can you remember about Kru and Tammy?

MARY. *(at a loss)* Tammy?

DANNY. *(patiently)* Tammy. Your daughter.

MARY. *(shakes her head, distraught)* Why can't I remember? Why is everything a total blank?

DANNY. It's simpler. You don't have to sift through and decide what to retain and what to forget. You just wipe the slate clean. But it's not hopeless, Mary. And it's not a permanent impairment. Not a disease.

MARY. Well, that's encouraging. At least I'm not sick.

MOTHER. *(enters)* Then why aren't you going?

MARY. *(turns and sees her)* I never said I was sick.

MOTHER. All your friends are going.

MARY. I don't want to go.

MOTHER. I don't believe that.

MARY. It doesn't interest me.

DANNY. Going where? What was she referring to?

MOTHER. How can it not interest you? Every girl wants to go to her prom!

MARY. I have no one to go with.

MOTHER. Don't tell me that. You're waiting for that house-painter.

MARY. Mother, I know it's hard to believe, but he actually has a name. Noel Kohler.

MOTHER. I don't know. Maybe you can meet someone else.

MARY. *(looking at her in amazement)* Someone else? Don't you like Noel?

MOTHER. I don't like his mother.

MARY. I'm not dating his mother.

MOTHER. Don't be too sure.

MARY. After we're married, she'll get to know the real me and she'll love me. And I'll love her. I'll call her "Mother Kohler." And she'll call me… she'll call me…

(turns to Danny, distressed)

Why can't I remember my own name?

DANNY. Because when you know what your name is, you'll know who you are.

MARY. When? When?

MOTHER. Maybe he's not the right boy. Maybe there's another boy…

MARY. Another boy? Never! There's nobody better than Noel! Nobody!

MOTHER. He's the only boy you ever dated. The only boy you know. There are other fish in the ocean.

MARY. Not for me. He's the only fish for me.

NOEL. *(dancing on)* La da da da dee… how do I look?

((He wears a white dinner jacket and carries a corsage box. **MOTHER** *leaves)*

MARY. Hey! You look beautiful! You look gorgeous! But you're supposed to say that about me.

NOEL. You look okay.

MARY. That's it?

NOEL. Fantastic! Stunning! Sooo pretty!

(hands her the corsage)

God! I can't believe it! It's finally here! Cissy, can you believe it? We're going to the prom!

MARY. *(turns to* **DANNY***)* Yes, yes! I remember! We were going to the prom! Of all the girls in school, he asked me. Me! How could I ever forget that? It was in June of… June… that was… that was… when was it?

DANNY. Don't you know?

MARY. How old am I?

(HE shrugs)

Well, can't you tell by my teeth? Or is that just with horses?

DANNY. When's your birthday?

MARY. May. When's yours?

NOEL. July twenty-six.

MARY. *(turning to him)* You'll be eighteen?

NOEL. Seventeen.

MARY. *(disappointed)* Oh. You're younger than me.

NOEL. And I always will be.

MARY. *(turning to **DANNY**)* I remember something. A smell.

DANNY. A smell? Good! Of what?

MARY. Paint. He worked in his father's paint store after school. His job was to mix the paints and his hands smelled of paint and turpentine and thinner. When we first went out on a date, it turned my stomach.

DANNY. And then?

MARY. Then. What do you think? I got to love the smell of paint.

NOEL. Can I ask you something?

MARY. Sure.

NOEL. I'd like to feel your breast tonight.

MARY. Tonight? We didn't even go out yet.

NOEL. I mean when we come home. I'd like to feel your breast when we get home from the prom.

MARY. God, Noel, talk about planning ahead. What did you do, figure out on prom night you were going to feel me up?

NOEL. Well, yeah.

MARY. I don't know.

*(**SHE** is silent. So is he)*

It's not terribly spontaneous. Why do you ask me?

NOEL. Maybe you don't want me to.

MARY. You know I like you.

NOEL. I like you.

MARY. Okay, so we'll go out tonight. And for the entire date I'll be a nervous wreck. No matter what we do, all I'll be thinking is at the end of the evening, you're going to touch my breast.

NOEL. Why don't I do it now and get it over with?

MARY. I don't think I can. Oh, God. What a bummer tonight's going to be.

DANNY. And was it?

MARY. No.

*(MUSIC begins. **MARY** takes **NOEL**'s arm and slowly **THEY** walk across the stage.)*

We were shy with each other, but we knew we were coming to a big moment in our relationship. I was afraid – but I was also excited. And then again, there was the possibility that I might throw up. That paint smell.

*(**THEY** stop walking. Stand for a moment just looking at each other. **NOEL** leans over and kisses her. It is not too short, not too long – and very sweet. Then, tentatively, reaches up his hand – lightly touches her breast. **SHE** puts her hand over his – and then he wraps his arms around her and **THEY** embrace)*

I still remember that night. It was such a surprise. It was so sweet. I didn't mind it at all. That was the surprise. That I liked it. I liked this boy…

*(**SHE** leans over to kiss him again. **NOEL** leaves)*

DANNY. Did you marry Noel Kohler? Is he the father of your daughter?

MARY. Daughter?

DANNY. Your daughter Tammy! What can you tell me about Tammy?

TAMMY. *(walking on)* I hate those stupid girls!

MARY. *(going to **TAMMY**)* What happened at the camp reunion?

TAMMY. Look, I don't want to talk about it.

MARY. You don't want to tell me?

TAMMY. I can't. I could never repeat it.

MARY. Something about you? About me?

TAMMY. No. About Kru.

MARY. Kru? What could it be?

TAMMY. There's something wrong.

MARY. Wrong?

MOTHER. *(entering)* Sure there's something wrong. What was this terrible thing I wanted for you!

MARY. But we had a wonderful dinner. Kru cooked. She's such a good cook. *(her face clouds)* But it was getting late. I had to go up and look for her.

DANNY. Yes? Go up where? Look for who?

MOTHER. *(entering)* Cele… help me out… don't let them keep me…

NOEL. *(entering)* I was thinking – maybe we should elope.

(MARY is pacing rapidly, frantically, circling the room, trying to block out these memories)

DANNY. Mary – what is it?

NOEL. It's got something to do with my mother.

KRU. *(entering)* There's so much about you I don't know.

(reaches over and takes her hand)

MARY. Oh. Oh!

(Mary starts to bring Kru's hand to her lips – then abruptly pulls her hand away, as from a flame. Rushes to her bed and starts putting on her sneakers)

DANNY. What are you doing?

MARY. I'm going for a run. I need some exercise.

DANNY. Mary – it's night.

MARY. That's all right. We joggers run at all hours. Neither rain nor sleet nor dark of night will keep us from cracking a shin or blistering a heel.

NOEL. It's got to do with my mother.

(exits)

DANNY. You know I can't let you out.

MARY. I've got to get out! Now let me out!

TAMMY. It was your decision!

    (*exits*)

DANNY. You're not ready, Mary! These things take time!

MARY. That's okay, I won't be long. Just twice around the track.

DANNY. Tomorrow.

MARY. Come on, Danny!

MOTHER. Cele! Help me out!

    (*exits*)

MARY. I've been here long enough! I haven't been crazy! You've been able to trust me! I need to run – now!

KRU. Tell them.

    (*exits*)

DANNY. I promise. First thing. Crack of dawn. I'll even go with you, Mary. I just can't let you out at night...

MARY. Why not? I've made remarkable progress! I know what the hell I'm doing. Now I need to run! Let me go!

DANNY. Where are you going?

MARY. I'm going to... I have to go to...

DANNY. A Hundred and Sixty-eighth Street?

MARY. Yes, yes!

DANNY. What's there? What is there, Mary?

MARY. I don't know. I need to make a phone call.

DANNY. A phone call? There's a phone here...

MARY. (*begging*) Please!

DANNY. Go ahead, make your call!

MARY. Okay. I'll use this phone.

DANNY. Good! Good!

MARY. You dial it.

DANNY. (*going to the phone*) Fine. Fine. What's the number?

MARY. Seven-one-eight...

DANNY. Seven-one-eight? *(turns to her)* That's a New York number. Brooklyn. Bronx. Riverdale.

MARY. That's right. Seven-one-eight. Five-four-eight-four oh five six.

DANNY. *(turning back to the phone)* Four... oh... five... eight... four oh five six...

(MARY comes up behind him and smashes him on the head with a pewter tray. DANNY cries out, clutches his head as momentarily stunned, HE reels, falls to the ground. MARY reaches into his pocket, pulls out the keys, rushes to the door and without even a glance at the injured DANNY unlocks the door and runs out of the room.)

End of Act One

ACT TWO

(Later. Mary's room. Danny is sitting in a chair, looking uncomfortable and quite dreary. Oleander is applying an ice pack to the back of Danny's head.)

DANNY. *(wincing)* Ow.

OLEANDER. Nice. Real nice.

(examining Danny's bruised head)

You probably have a mild concussion.

DANNY. No, I don't. I have no blurred vision, no nausea, I'm obviously alert and intelligent...

OLEANDER. Check it anyway. It wouldn't hurt to get a CAT-scan.

DANNY. I don't think she wanted to kill me.

OLEANDER. *(wryly)* Really?

DANNY. *(gingerly touching the back of his head)* She didn't even break the skin.

OLEANDER. True. All your bleeding is inside your skull. You're getting close. Fugue... the closer you get, the harder she runs.

DANNY. Don't patronize me, Ollie, I know what fugue is. This latest fugue episode just confirms her fears

OLEANDER. All right. So what's causing the fear?

DANNY. Guilt. Remorse. Or loss. Anger. Or simply pain. I'm getting on rough territory. Why is she running? What did I touch? Tammy? Where is Tammy? With her father? Could she be dead?

OLEANDER. It's possible.

DANNY. Oh, fuck, everything's possible.

OLEANDER. She told you she needed to make a phone call. And she gave you the number.

DANNY. Yes. A New York number.

OLEANDER. Did you check it out?

(Danny looks at him. Then picks up the phone, dials)

DANNY. It's ringing. *(beat)* And ringing. And ringing.

OLEANDER. No voice mail?

(Danny shrugs, listens a little longer, then hangs up)

DANNY. It's a working number. Somebody's phone.

OLEANDER. Maybe her mother.

DANNY. Her mother? Her mother is dead.

OLEANDER. Maybe. She wants to phone her mother. Something is telling her this can't be. She doesn't want to hear it, she doesn't want to learn more, she can't bear the pain of facing that loss again. So she wanders. She's running away from the truth of her mother's death – and at the same time, she's wandering in search of her mother.

DANNY. You think that's it?

OLEANDER. No.

DANNY. *(rubbing his head)* I don't know how she lives. How she supports herself. Does she have another life? Another family? Is that where she's running to?

OLEANDER. Or maybe she just went away to die.

DANNY. Oh, Jesus.

OLEANDER. But erasing the memory is a form of suicide, isn't it?

DANNY. But what if she starts to remember? What if she kills herself then? That's possible, isn't it?

OLEANDER. I would speculate that in Mary's case, "going away" takes the place of dying. Once she's on the move, the death wish has to subside. *(slight pause)* I don't think suicide is likely.

*(**DANNY** doesn't answer)*

Okay?

DANNY. It's happening again, isn't it? Good old history. Up to its old snide trick of repeating itself.

OLEANDER. It's not happening again!

DANNY. Smart ass that I was. So smart! I knew it all! Why shouldn't I know it all? Wasn't I the best, the top, the fucking pinnacle! Who was better than Danny

Lucchesi? The street kid with the smarts, brimming with scholarships, top of the class! Who would have guessed I'd be a fuck up!

OLEANDER. We all fuck up one time or another...

DANNY. Oh, what the hell do you know! It's always been downhill for you, John Oleander the Third, or is it the Fourth. Waltzing into Johns Hopkins on the backs of Doctor Daddy and Doctor Granddaddy and Surgeon General great-Granddaddy, grand old alumni! What do you know about fucking up! It's not in your fucking genes!

(He turns away and fumes for a minute. Oleander lets him)

OLEANDER. Feel better?

DANNY. I'm sorry.

OLEANDER. No, you're not.

DANNY. Yeah, yeah, I am. You don't deserve that, Ollie. It's not your fault that you were born rich.

OLEANDER. Or that you were born smart.

DANNY. Sure. Not even a year in practice and I knew it all! So certain, so positive. You're finished, Philip, my friend, you're all cured, all better, so go on home and stick a knife in her belly!

OLEANDER. Danny, it's been four years! And none of your gargantuan guilt is going to bring her back.

(putting on his coat)

Come on, we'd better get you to the ER. If we get a trace of her, I'll let you know right away. The police have been notified as well as the Transit Authority, bus terminals, airports...

DANNY. She has no money. She has no I.D. She's wearing a jogging suit.

OLEANDER. So is half the city. I wouldn't be too optimistic about her coming back. After all, she's been wandering for months, years, perhaps. We'll never know how many...

(HE stops as the door opens and **MARY** *enters.* **OLE-ANDER** *and* **DANNY** *exchange looks.* **OLEANDER** *immediately gets up and leaves)*

DANNY. Enjoy your walk?

MARY. It's starting to rain.

DANNY. Is that why you came back?

MARY. Not altogether.

(sitting down)

My feet hurt.

DANNY. Really? I wish I could be properly sympathetic. But my head hurts.

MARY. Your head hurts?

DANNY. Thanks to you.

MARY. Thanks to me? *(remembering)* Oh, Danny! What did I do! Are you all right?

DANNY. I have, what you might call, a swelled head.

MARY. Oh, Danny! I'm so sorry! Should you see a doctor?

DANNY. What for? I haven't lost my memory. What the hell, Mary! I thought we were friends.

MARY. We are friends. I'm glad to see you. Really glad to see you.

DANNY. Terrific.

MARY. Aren't you glad to see me?

DANNY. *(yelling)* That's not the point!

(the yelling hurts his head)

Ow!

MARY. Don't be mad at me. I'm cold and I'm wet. And my feet hurt. I need a hug. *(beat)* How about it?

(Pause. Then **DANNY** *gets up. Walks over to her, wraps his arms around her. Hugs her hard.)*

DANNY. Why did you run away?

MARY. I don't know.

DANNY. The telephone number you didn't want me to call – did you call it?

MARY. No.

DANNY. Why not?

MARY. It happens every time. I go to a phone booth. I remember the number. Then something gets in the way. I don't have change. Or the phone isn't working. And I forget the number again.

(stops)

DANNY. Why did you come back?

MARY. I told you. My feet hurt.

(sits down, starts unlacing her shoes)

My feet always hurt. I remember that.

(takes off one shoe, gently massages her foot)

You people who have never tramped from showroom to showroom will never know the agony of really sore feet!

*(**KRU** walks in carrying a basin)*

KRU. Put them in here.

MARY. Oh, damn it! God damn it!

DANNY. What is it?

MARY. Nothing!

KRU. I've put in some salts. Your feet will feel marvelous.

DANNY. *(violently)* Come on!

MARY. I don't remember! What do you want me to do, make it up?

DANNY. I don't believe you! I don't believe you don't remember! You remember something! If you didn't, you wouldn't have clobbered me. Now tell me!

MARY. Oh, damn you! I tell you everything! And you don't tell me anything! What about you, Danny? What's your story?

DANNY. Never mind my story. That's not what we're here for.

MARY. Not fair! What kind of friend keeps secrets?

DANNY. What are you remembering? Right now! Right now! What is it?

MARY. I don't know!

DANNY. What is it!

KRU. The water's just the right temperature.

MARY. *(to DANNY)* It's your fault!

(turning to KRU)

Your fault, Kru.

KRU. My fault? You told me you loved to walk.

MARY. *(sits on couch, puts her feet in the basin)*
I meant to the corner and back. Not fifteen miles before lunch. Look at that. Is that a bunion?

KRU. We've got to get you in shape for Europe.

MARY. My God, it's a bunion!...

KRU. Walking is the only way to see Europe. And if it's really too much for you and your poor feet, we'll rest up sitting at the concert in Salzberg. And the opera in Milan. Maybe even a gondola in Venice. Sipping expresso along the Cote d'Azur –Nice, St. Paul de Vence, Cap D'Antibes...

MARY. Oh, dear, all those names! It's sinful that I haven't been out of this country!

KRU. So? You've probably seen more of America than most of us.

MARY. Big deal. Showrooms and hotel rooms.

KRU. Cocktail lounges?

MARY. Comes with the territory.

KRU. Lots of dates?

MARY. Comes with the territory.

KRU. Anyone special?

MARY. Oh. A couple. Here and there. *(laughs)* One of the other buyers was filling out an application for something. And where it said "sex", he wrote, "once in Peoria."

(Kru laughs)

Actually, it was with me.

KRU. Oh? *(beat)* In Peoria?

MARY. In Peoria, Illinois.

KRU. When was that?

MARY. Well… how old is Tammy?

KRU. Why didn't you marry him?

MARY. His wife got there first. It doesn't matter. Hey, I have Tammy!

(to Danny)

Yes! This one I was going to have!

(Mother walks on)

MARY *(continuing; to Danny)* Of course, I had to tell her. It took me a long time. I thought she'd throw me into a home, a prison, the gutter. I worried and fretted and pondered and agonized and finally I told her. Well. She was a giant.

MOTHER. You'll have your baby. We'll get a bigger apartment. I'll take out a loan. I'll help you raise it.

MARY. A giant. *(pause)* So naturally I figured I could tell her anything.

(Mother exits)

KRU. Dinner's almost ready. Drink?

MARY. No, no, I couldn't. What kind of drink?

KRU. I'm having a vermouth cassis.

(goes to the bar to fix it)

MARY. Yes? What a good idea. I always want what you're having. It always looks so good. You're so visual, Kru. A sprig of mint in your iced tea. Those clinking ice cubes and that lovely amber color and that's all I want in life, iced tea, iced tea!

KRU. Here's your vermouth cassis.

MARY. Yes, yes, that's all I want in life, a vermouth cassis!

KRU. You're easy to please.

(She starts to massage Mary's foot. Mary closes her eyes)

When you come back from your next trip, I'm going to pick you up at the airport.

MARY. Oh, no, no. It's out of your way.

KRU. Doesn't matter.

MARY. It'll be rush hour. You'll get into that horrible traffic. I can take a cab, the bus...

KRU. You can tell me about your trip. We'll stop for a bite of dinner. I don't mind it at all.

MARY. *(touching Kru's head)* How sweet. How awfully sweet.

(turns to Danny)

Can you imagine? Going all the way to the airport? In rush hour?

KRU. You know, when Tammy goes to college, you could move in here. There's plenty of room.

MARY. Kru...

KRU. You know I want you to.

(Mary doesn't answer)

Don't you want to?

MARY. Do I want to? Every time I walk into your place, my body sighs.

KRU. Well?

MARY. There's my mother – she hasn't been well lately... she's getting so frail. The doctor thinks she should go to the hospital for a few days so they can do some tests.

KRU. But what about you? What's left for you?

MARY. This. Being here. It's the only time I feel permanent. The rest of it – it's like I'm still sitting on empty packing boxes. My life is so temporary. Never quite there yet. Always waiting.

KRU. For what?

MARY. I don't know. Husband, family, home.

KRU. There are other ways to be happy.

*(**MARY** just looks at her.)*

DANNY. You don't have to stop.

KRU. I'm very happy now. I don't think I could be happier. What about you? Are you happy?

(Mary doesn't answer)

DANNY. Can you tell me how you were feeling? Can you remember that?

MARY. It was so easy. I was sharing with Kru all the things I'd always planned on sharing...

(stops)

DANNY. Yes?

MARY. ... with a man. But with Kru – it was as though I kept saying, "This doesn't really count."

KRU. Oh, yes. It counts.

(SHE leaves)

MARY. I loved making plans with her. There were so many things to do. We were going to Europe. Wonderful places. Cote d'Azur... Nice... St. Paul de Vence... Cap d'Antibes...

MOTHER. *(entering)* This summer we're going to Far Rockaway. I found a place one block from the Boardwalk.

MARY. A place? You mean a room with two beds and a table?

MOTHER. So what if we share a kitchen. You can hear the ocean at night.

MARY. That's not the ocean, Mother. That's somebody's toilet flushing.

MOTHER. The sound of the waves makes me sleep like a baby! Nothing like the ocean! The salt water rewitalizes you!

NOEL. *(entering, wearing shorts)* Far Rockaway? How will I get there? It's an hour and a half by subway!

MOTHER. *(to MARY)* Tell him he can sleep over. Tell him he can breathe the air

(SHE exits)

NOEL. Sleep over? What about my mother?

MARY. Tell her you can breathe the air.

NOEL. I hate thinking of September. You'll be here and I'll be in Chicago.

DANNY. *(sharply)* Chicago?

TAMMY. *(appearing)* Why can't I go to college here? I don't want to go to school in Chicago.

DANNY. Chicago!

(TAMMY leaves)

MARY. *(wheeling on DANNY, annoyed)* Why do you keep saying Chicago? How do you expect me to remember if you constantly interrupt me?

NOEL. Four years! How will we make it?

MARY. You'll probably forget me by the end of your freshman year. Out of sight, out of mind.

NOEL. Ha, that's what my mother hopes. Then I remind her that you and your Mom haven't exactly forgotten your father even though he's in Pilgrim State…

(And he stops)

MARY. *(looks at him, stunned)* You told her?

NOEL. Oh, shit.

MARY. My secret.

NOEL. *(maybe he looks away)* She knew anyway. It wasn't a surprise. She really knew. I guess a lot of people knew. She told me first. She brought it up.

(but he is mortified)

Shit. I'm sorry… I'm sorry. Oh, God, Cissy… you're shivering. Let me hold you.

(leading her to the bed)

Lie down with me. I'll keep you warm. I'll stay with you. Forever. Forever.

*(**HE** takes her under the blankets)*

*(Lights fade. Light up on **DANNY**)*

DANNY. You went to bed with Noel? You got pregnant? But not with Tammy? Tammy was later. But what about Noel? Where is he? Did you marry him? Is he alive? Can you tell me, Mary?

MARY. Tell you?

(Lights up on the bed. **NOEL** *is gone)*

KRU. *(entering)* You're making it harder on yourself. Just tell them.

MARY. *(turning to her)* Tell them?

KRU. Don't you want to live here? With me?

MARY. Oh, God. It's all I want.

(Kru smiles – and leaves. The memory is gone.)

DANNY. Did you stay? Did you move in with Kru? Do you remember that? Any of it?

MARY. *(abruptly facing him)* Listen. I keep asking you. Tell me about yourself. What's your story?

DANNY. Now let's not start that...

MARY. I tell you everything and you don't tell me anything. It's not fair!

DANNY. I'm a doctor. I don't have to be fair.

MARY. Where were you born? How many brothers and sisters do you have? How many mothers and fathers? Was your father a doctor, too?

DANNY. My father – a doctor? *(laughs)* My Dad was an elevator operator.

MARY. Well, that's interesting. Tell me about him.

DANNY. Old ploy. Patient turning the subject around – it's called "avoidance".

MARY. Maybe I just want to know about your father.

DANNY. Maybe it's your father you want to know about.

MARY. I asked you first.

DANNY. My father. Okay. Talked a lot. Ungrammatical. Never cracked a book. Favorite sport was watching boxing on TV. Liked to eat, drink a little. I was the only child. He was my best friend. I think I was his. He didn't see me get my college degree. He didn't see me get my medical degree. He didn't see me graduate at the top of my class. But I did it all for him. Okay. Tell me about your father.

MARY. Sure. Why not? If he had been around, I would have been rich, desirable, my teeth straightened, my nose fixed, my hair bleached, my breasts enlarged, a strong daddy around to interview my suitors and let them know I'm a prize.

DANNY. You are a prize.

MARY. Okay, sure.

DANNY. I think you're a prize.

MARY. You don't count.

DANNY. What made him sick? Was it you?

MARY. What?

DANNY. What terrible thing did you do that sent him off the deep end?

MARY. Nothing! What are you, nuts? I was a little girl, seven, eight, ten maybe. What the hell could I have done?

DANNY. But you hated him, didn't you? You hated him for leaving you and your mother in the lurch, didn't you?

MARY. No! I loved him!

DANNY. How could you love him? He deserted you, didn't he?

MARY. You're a creep!

DANNY. Then what are you so angry about?

MARY. Oh, go to hell! You bastard!

(still fuming – then, softening)

I adored him. What I remember of him. What do I remember? The way he woke me. I can close my eyes and almost feel it happening. He would touch my face. Softly, gently. And he would say, "Hey, there. It's time to wake up. Everybody's waiting for you. The birds – the sun -the day. Nothing can get started till you get up."

(turning to **DANNY***)*

Do you know what was the matter with him? He was afraid an airplane was going to hit him. An airplane was going to fall out of the sky and hit him.

DANNY. Agoraphobia...

MARY. Oh, who cares! WHO CARES! The point is he was afraid an airplane was going to hit him and for that stupid reason, she didn't want me to go out with her son!

DANNY. There's a lot of injustice in this world.

MARY. Okay.

DANNY. There may have been extenuating...

MARY. Go fuck yourself!

DANNY. I'm only playing devil's advo...

MARY. Well, don't play devil's advocate! Be my advocate! Why isn't anybody for me? For me!

MOTHER. *(walking on, carrying a vase)* I have something for you. A waz.

MARY. A what?

MOTHER. *(puts the vase on the table)* Somebody had a fire and they threw this beautiful waz out the window.

MARY. A what?

MOTHER. How do you pronounce it, waz or waze?

MARY. *(after a moment)* Waze.

MOTHER. A beautiful waze. For your new apartment.

MARY. *(filled with gratitude)* Oh, Mom! Mother! How thoughtful! How kind!

(goes over and hugs her)

Then it's okay! You're okay about my moving!

MOTHER. I'm not okay. Why leave this nice apartment? We have so much room here.

MARY. Oh, Mom. Don't you think I'm a little old to be living with my mother? And with Tammy going off to college, it's a good time for me to get some new surroundings.

MOTHER. Don't you ever plan to get married? It's never too late, you know.

MARY. Well, of course I plan to get married. Everybody gets married.

(*pause. Then, tentatively*)

I don't know. Maybe not. Maybe there are other ways for me to be happy.

MOTHER. Other ways? What other ways?

MARY. What if I told you I met somebody.

MOTHER. Ah! What joy! You met somebody! Who? Who is he?

(*Mary opens her mouth. Then closes it*)

MARY. Will you be all right? Will you be all right living alone, all by yourself? But don't worry, I'll come to visit. We'll go out for dinner, see a show…

MOTHER. Never mind about me. I've lived my life. I don't know how much longer I'll be around. I just want you to be happy.

MARY. Well, that's a sure way to make me happy, telling me you're going to kick the bucket any second. I want you to go to the hospital. The doctor wants to do some tests.

MOTHER. I don't like hospitals. They make you sick.

MARY. I worry about you.

MOTHER. Likewise.

MARY. I'll be fine! I intend to read, listen to music, exercise, travel. There's a pool there, where I'm moving. They keep it toasty warm, even in winter. Tammy will love that when she comes home on vacation.

MOTHER. It's no fun being alone.

MARY. I won't be alone.

MOTHER. No? Who will you have?

MARY. I'll get a cat.

(**MOTHER** *leaves.* **MARY** *turns to* **DANNY**)

Somebody told me you can learn a great deal from a

cat. Just observe. So I got a cat and I sat and watched it for days. And I learned nothing. Okay, maybe I learned to wash after every meal, but that's it.

DANNY. What was the cat's name?

(MARY *thinks. Shakes her head. Can't remember*)

Was it Tammy?

(MARY *looks at him. After a moment, HE leaves.*)

(*Lights down on Mary's room, up on doctors' area.* OLE-ANDER *waits for him*)

OLEANDER. Why did you ask her that?

DANNY. Why not? Maybe there is no Tammy. Maybe it's all a scam.

OLEANDER. Why do you want to think that?

DANNY. Because I've got to think of everything! Every option, every curve until I can be sure. Or at least, reasonably sure.

OLEANDER. Are you sure of anything?

DANNY. Yeah. The guilt. That lousy, useless, destructive guilt. That's my diagnosis, Ollie. Fugue is due to the patient being overcome by guilt from which she cannot escape. She's capable of remembering. She simply can't bear the guilt of whatever the hell she did. Or thinks she did.

OLEANDER. You realize we'll be transferring her in three days.

DANNY. Where?

OLEANDER. Someplace more suitable for long-term care.

DANNY. Why don't you pull some of your important strings. Get an extension.

OLEANDER. Why?

DANNY. I don't know. You may not want to hear this.

OLEANDER. I'm sure I don't.

DANNY. Look, Ollie. If it's so painful, so devastating that rather than remember, she prefers to forget everything – why force her to remember?

OLEANDER. Force her to remember?

DANNY. I know it's a novel idea to a psychiatrist – but maybe – just maybe – she's better off the way she is!

OLEANDER. Are you for real?

DANNY. We teach stroke victims how to talk again.

OLEANDER. Yeah, we do.

DANNY. They don't sound the way they did. The regional dialect is gone. They talk exactly as the speech therapist talks. But they talk again. She doesn't have to be Cecilia Schooner. She can be Mary Smith – and have a whole new set of memories.

OLEANDER. You want to give her a whole new set of memories?

DANNY. She can't live with the ones she has. Why can't she stay the way she is?

OLEANDER. The way she is? You think she's a charming, unusual woman? The patient is an amnesiac. She roams the subways and streets, walks until her feet are blistered and bloodied, has no connection at all with reality. When she gets too close to a memory, she's driven to get away from it – at any cost. The cost to you was a concussion. Next time, she might kill you.

DANNY. But what if it's a memory she can't live with?

OLEANDER. It's the guilt she can't live with! You know about that, don't you, Danny? But once the guilt is assuaged, she'll be stronger. Maybe she won't be as interesting, this vague smiling woman with no past. She'll have a whole other life, probably a life with no room in it for you…

DANNY. Oh, come on!

OLEANDER. But that's your job, Doctor. To put her back into that life.

DANNY. I'm doing what I can, Ollie. Then I'm out of here.

OLEANDER. Don't give me that shit. I know what's bugging you. You got yourself involved with your patient.

DANNY. Fuck you.

OLEANDER. You can't separate it, can you? You can't remember that you are Doctor Lucchesi and she is the goddam patient!

DANNY. Listen, don't you analyze me, you prick!

OLEANDER. Then get in there and help the lady!

DANNY. Don't push me!

OLEANDER. Do your goddam job!

(*Beat. They glare at each other*)

DANNY. (*quietly*) What if I told you I was afraid.

OLEANDER. What if I told you we're all afraid.

(*Danny gets up and leaves. Lights up in Mary's room as Danny enters*)

DANNY. So how's the jogging coming?

MARY. Oh, great. I jog around that track, around and around and around and I wait for my heart attack.

DANNY. It's really good for you...

MARY. Sure, sure. Anyway, the best part of my jogging is I always plan to run around the track twenty-five times. But naturally, I can't remember how many times I run around. So for all I know, I may have run around fifty times. A hundred times. I may have run the twenty-six mile marathon. I may have won the twenty-six mile marathon.

DANNY. (*after a moment*) Don't you trust me, Mary?

MARY. Oh, I don't know. You're such a mystery.

DANNY. (*laughs*) I'm a mystery?

MARY. I might trust you a little more if I knew you a little better. And I would like you a lot more if you didn't keep nagging me.

DANNY. Nagging you?

MARY. Yes! Remember, remember! I can't remember. I simply can't remember.

DANNY. I think you can. I think you don't want to.

MARY. And what makes you know all the answers?

DANNY. I don't know all the answers. I know all the questions.

MARY. You're cute, Danny. And nice. That's why I'm helping you. I'm going to do everything I can to make your book a best-seller.

DANNY. My book will never be a best-seller. It has no pictures.

MARY. I'll let you take blown-up photos of me and my damaged brain. You can go on all the talk shows.

DANNY. Your brain isn't damaged. But mine may be, thanks to you.

MARY. *(remorseful)* Why did I do that? Why did I hit you?

DANNY. Because you felt trapped.

MARY. Trapped? By what?

DANNY. By a memory. Or a wish.

MARY. A wish?

DANNY. Could be. A totally unacceptable wish. A wish you might not even be conscious of. But if you were, it would fill you with shame.

MARY. A wish. Just a wish? But did it come true?

DANNY. Maybe.

MARY. How terrible! What in the world could I have wished for? Am I so bad? Am I so awful?

DANNY. No. I don't think you're awful. You know I like you, Mary.

MARY. How can you like me? I'm some kind of a crazy lady, a bag lady, a derelict, a wanderer. You might find me good material for your book. But this isn't really me.

DANNY. I like what I know about you now. You're fun, you're interesting, you're…

(he stops)

MARY. You've got it backwards, Danny. Isn't it the patient who falls in love with the doctor?

DANNY. I almost didn't know you. I could have stayed in my room. I wouldn't have met you.

MARY. What were you doing in your room? Why weren't you out being a doctor?

DANNY. It happens to some of us. We're terrific students, we get our diplomas, we start our practice – and right off the bat, we do something wrong.

MARY. Wrong?

DANNY. Really wrong.

KRU. *(walks on)* I want you to live with me.

MARY. It's impossible.

KRU. Anything else is impossible.

TAMMY. *(entering)* What's going on, Mom?

MARY. *(turning to her)* What's going on?

DANNY. I thought someone was well. And he wasn't.

MARY. And?

DANNY. Someone got hurt.

MARY. *(impatiently)* Well, what happened?

DANNY. I don't know if I should tell you...

TAMMY. I can't tell you.

MARY. Forget it. Keep your big secret. Who gives a damn!

KRU. I told her it was no secret.

MARY. I'm sick of secrets!

TAMMY. I don't want to go there for dinner.

DANNY. I had this patient. Panphobic. Fear of everything, inside, outside, elevators, cars, people, dogs. He needed to belong. I became his friend, brought him to my home for an occasional dinner, made him feel part of the family. He responded, was getting better, better, better. One day all better.

KRU. You owe them that much. They love you. It will be fine.

DANNY. I told him he was finished with treatment. I discharged him. He left my office, went home, got a knife and... and... he stabbed... he stabbed...

MARY. He stabbed himself!

DANNY. He stabbed my wife.

MARY. Oh, God.

DANNY. I'm sorry. I'm sorry.

MARY. Oh, yes, yes! That's a real secret!

NOEL. *(walking on)* It makes me feel closer to you. I know something nobody else knows. That's special.

*(Lights out. **DANNY** walks out and into Doctors' area, where **OLEANDER** waits, furious)*

OLEANDER. Are you out of your fucking mind?

DANNY. I don't know. What do you think?

OLEANDER. Why did you do that!

DANNY. Why not? I'm asking her to reveal all her secrets! Why shouldn't I tell her mine?

OLEANDER. Danny! You're her doctor! You're supposed to be uninvolved!

DANNY. Oh, shit! Why should I be? I'm in my own fugue state, damn it! The only problem is I can remember! Damn it! I can remember!

(Long pause. Oleander waits)

Did you know I was planning to leave her?

OLEANDER. *(after a moment)* I think I knew you weren't happy.

DANNY. She broke her back for me. Worked every day while I took my classes. Rushed home every night to cook my dinner which I gobbled so I could spend the rest of the night all by myself studying. Then when it was all over and I was a doctor and we were ready to reap the harvest, I didn't want her anymore.

OLEANDER. Was there someone else?

DANNY. Dozens of someone elses. I hadn't met them yet. But I couldn't – as long as she was around.

(turns to Oleander)

So listen, Doc. The thought comes to me every so often. Did I do that to make it easy for me? Did I break all the rules with Philip Belzer so he could wind up getting rid of her for me? I can't help wondering…

OLEANDER. *(appalled)* Jesus! Is that what you've been carrying? Danny, why didn't you talk to someone? Why didn't you talk to me? Why didn't you talk to anyone?

(Lights up on Mary's room. Zelda is there)

ZELDA. I think you've made a lot of progress, Cele. You seem so much better.

MARY. Yes, I feel so much better.

ZELDA. Do you?

MARY. No. I feel the same.

ZELDA. I don't agree. I think you feel better and you just don't want to admit it.

MARY. Well, Zelda, you know best.

ZELDA. *(rummaging through the CD's)* Oh, look at this. Do you ever play these?

MARY. What?

ZELDA. Did you get them from your mother?

MARY. No.

ZELDA. I bet you did! What oldies! Yes, I remember this! You loved this song. I remember it was your mother's favorite song.

MARY. My mother's?

ZELDA. You don't remember it?

MARY. No.

ZELDA. *(singing)* "Oh, green eyes with their soft lights... Those eyes that promise sweet nights... "

MARY. Yes, yes, I remember, I remember!

ZELDA. You do?

MARY. No. I just hate to hear you sing.

ZELDA. *(hurt)* I don't understand it, Cele. We were such good friends. And now you act as though you don't like me at all.

MARY. It's not an act. I don't like you at all.

ZELDA. You were always angry at me. You knew about me and Noel.

MARY. Noel?

ZELDA. You knew I always liked him. You knew that, didn't you? You knew I came to Chicago to be with him.

MARY. Chicago?

ZELDA. But he quit college. He broke his mother's heart. He wasn't the same after you. He was never the same.

MARY. Who?

ZELDA. He let me stay with him but he never really wanted me. I'm the one who should be angry! Poor Noel. He was so young. Personally, I think you lost your memory when Noel died.

MARY. Noel?

(Suddenly, Mary picks up a sneaker and throws it at the wall.)

ZELDA. Hey! What's the matter with you?

MARY. You can't hold on to it! You can't keep harping on every dumb senseless thing that ever happened! What's the point? What's the point anyway?

ZELDA. What do you mean? What's the point of what?

MARY. Of anything! ANYTHING! So you write it in your diary! And you press your corsage! So you remember! So what!

ZELDA. You're weird! You were always weird! Probably inherited your nuttiness from your father!

MARY. *(suddenly furious)* Get out of here! Get out of my life!

ZELDA. Your life? Ha! What life?

(Mary grabs the other sneaker. Zelda runs out of the room.)

MARY. So you remember! So what? It happened! It's past! It's finished! It's no more... no more!

(Music begins – Trio singing)

TRIO.

WHEN I HEAR THAT SERENADE IN BLUE
I'M SOMEWHERE IN ANOTHER WORLD
ALONE WITH YOU...

(**MARY** *goes to closet, starts putting on scarf.* **MOTHER** *enters, sits at table*)

MOTHER. Why do you pick the coldest day of the year to go out?

MARY. Noel is coming over.

MOTHER. Noel? What is he doing home? It's not even a holiday.

MARY. I don't know.

MOTHER. Look, honey, maybe you want to go to the movies with me?

MARY. *(looks oddly at her* **MOTHER***)* Look, "honey"? Didn't I tell you Noel was on his way over?

MOTHER. Sure.

MARY. So why would I want to go to the movies? I'm aching to see Noel. It's almost a miracle that he came home now, now, now of all times! Yes, that's just what it is – a miracle!

(**MOTHER** *just shrugs.* **NOEL** *walks on downstage.* **HE** *wears a heavy winter jacket and looks very cold.* **MARY** *runs over to him and embraces him*)

MARY *(CONT'D)* God, you're freezing! Just being near you makes me cold.

NOEL. I walked over.

MARY. What are you doing home? You didn't tell me you were coming in this weekend.

NOEL. I have to talk to you. Let's go for a walk.

MARY. What's wrong with your face? It's all broken out. Do you have your period?

(HE doesn't answer)

Okay, now you ask me.

NOEL. Ask you what?

MARY. I'm not broken out. Get it? *(laughs)* You don't get it.

NOEL. We've got to talk.

MARY. Yes, we do. I have something to tell you.

NOEL. What is it?

MARY. You go first.

NOEL. Okay.

> (**THEY** *walk out. Immediately* **SHE** *starts shivering.*
> **THEY** *walk for a while*)
>
> My mother is driving me crazy. She won't quit bugging
> me.

MARY. About me?

NOEL. That's right. That's why they sent me to Chicago.
They thought if I was away at school, I'd forget you.

> (*finally*)
>
> I can't take it anymore, Cissy.

MARY. Does it have to do with my father?

NOEL. That's part of it.

MARY. That's all of it.

NOEL. No, that's part of it.

MARY. That's stupid.

NOEL. It's keeping me from working. I mean, this tension,
this nagging all the time. I can't concentrate. My head,
it just hurts all the time. I never told you everything,
but the pressure's getting to me.

> (*They are silent for a while*)
>
> Maybe we shouldn't see each other for a while. I feel
> guilty, you know. I mean, they're sending me to col-
> lege. I guess I should concentrate on my work.
>
> (*Silence again*)
>
> Say something.

MARY. I can't think of what to say. I can't even think of what
to think.

> (*turns to* **DANNY**)
>
> So this is how it happens. This is how love stories end.
> You go for a walk and he tells you he can't take it any-
> more. It isn't a discussion. It's a telling. I'm telling you
> I can't take it anymore. The tension. The nagging. I

feel guilty. They're sending me to college.

DANNY. Is that what you said?

MARY. No. I said okay.

NOEL. *(turning to look at her)* What?

MARY. *(to* NOEL*)* Okay. We better go back. It's freezing.

NOEL. What did you want to tell me?

MARY. Nothing.

NOEL. *(looks at her)* Nothing?

MARY. Well. It's nothing now.

NOEL. I was planning to give you a ring on your birthday.

MARY. I know. I was planning to take it. *(softly)* I guess we plan too much.

NOEL. Take care of yourself.

MARY. Yeah. You, too, Noel.

> *(***HE*** walks away. Mother enters. She looks very sad.)*

Look how sad you are. It's true about mothers. You knew what Noel was saying to me out there?

MOTHER. I just heard from the hospital. Daddy's not coming home.

MARY. No? Not ever?

MOTHER. Never.

> *(She leaves)*

MARY. *(to Danny)* That's not fair, is it? We've been waiting for him to come home, all these years. Once he came home, everything would fall into place. Everything would be just fine. Daddy would make everything all better.

TAMMY. *(walking on)* Where were you tonight, Mom?

MARY. *(at kitchen counter, pouring herself some milk)* I was... where were you?

TAMMY. What are you so worried about, Mom?

MARY. Never mind. I know, I know every young woman wants to keep a part of herself a mystery. At least that's what Voltaire said.

TAMMY. Voltaire?

MARY. It was either Voltaire – or Jackie Kennedy's father.

TAMMY. So where were you?

MARY. *(joining her at the table)* I was… working on my trip to Europe. When you're away at school this Fall – I thought I might finally take a trip to Europe.

TAMMY. Who are you going with?

MARY. Oh, I don't know. I thought I'd go with… maybe a tour.

TAMMY. You going with Kru?

MARY. Kru? What makes you think I'd be going with Kru?

TAMMY. That's who I'd go with. Kru knows Europe. I'd certainly want my first trip to be with someone who knows the place.

MARY. Yes. Well, that makes sense. I suppose that's a good idea but… well, I don't know if Kru's about to go to Europe…

TAMMY. She is.

MARY. *(startled)* She is?

TAMMY. She told me she's going.

MARY. When?

TAMMY. *(lightly)* When did she tell me or when is she going?

MARY. *(takes a breath)* As a matter of fact, that's where I was tonight. Over at Kru's place.

TAMMY. I see. I guess I won't be going to Europe with you. The two of you.

MARY. But… you'll be away at school.

TAMMY. Right.

MARY. She's invited us for dinner… Kru has. I thought it would be good for us to get out.

TAMMY. I'm getting out. I'll be away at school.

MARY. Yes, that's the reason for the dinner. A little farewell get-together.

TAMMY. I don't want to go.

MARY. Look, she wants to cook dinner for us…

TAMMY. Leave me out.

MARY. *(slight pause. She takes a breath)* I want you to know something. I think I could be happy now. It's taken me a long time. *(She hesitates)* But things have changed. Things are different. There's someone who I want to share my life with. Someone who's made all the difference…

TAMMY. What is it, Mom? You met somebody? You met a guy? You're getting married? I'll have a Dad? *(beat)* Is that it, Mom? Is that what you're telling me?

MARY. *(pause – then walks behind **TAMMY**, puts her arms around her)*

Let's have dinner at Kru's, Tammy. With Grandma gone now, it's just the two of us. I really need you to come with me. We deserve a little break. You know what a fabulous cook Kru is. It'll be fun.

(Tammy takes Mary's arms off and walks out)

TRIO. *(singing)*
SHARING ALL THE DREAMS
WE USED TO KNOW
MANY MOONS AGO…

*(Mary goes to the couch, stretches out. **KRU** enters. Goes to bar, pours two brandies. Brings one to **MARY**. Sits on arm of couch, picks up records)*

KRU. Why do you like to play these old records?

*(**MARY** shrugs. **KRU** stands up, holds out her arms to **MARY**)*

Dance with me.

*(**MARY** doesn't move.)*

It's all right. Come on, Cecilia. Dance with me.

TRIO.
ONCE AGAIN YOUR FACE COMES BACK TO ME.
JUST LIKE THE THEME
OF SOME FORGOTTEN MELODY…

(Reluctantly, but unable to resist, **MARY** *allows* **KRU** *to put her arms around her and lead her in a slow dance. After a few moments,* **MARY** *shakes her head sadly and breaks away.)*

KRU. It's all right. It really is.

DANNY. What is it?

MARY. Nothing!

TRIO.

> IN THE ALBUM OF MY MEMORY
> SERENADE IN BLUE...

DANNY. Come on, what is it?

(Mary's head is down. **SHE** *is crying)*

MARY. I don't know. I'm allowed to cry.

TRIO.

> IT SEEMS LIKE ONLY YESTERDAY
> A SMALL CAFE, A CROWDED FLOOR
> AND AS WE DANCED THE NIGHT AWAY
> I HEARD YOU SAY, "FOREVER MORE"

KRU. Don't you want to stay? Don't you want to be with me?

MARY. It's all I want. But it's impossible.

KRU. Anything else is impossible. Just tell them.

*(***KRU*** leaves)*

MARY. *(to the exiting* **KRU***)* You don't understand. Everybody gets married. It's part of life, you grow up, you go to school, you get married. It's the most natural thing in the world.

MOTHER. *(entering)* Then don't get married. I am not pushing you.

MARY. *(turning to her)* I need to tell you why.

MOTHER. No, you don't.

MARY. It isn't easy for me to tell you...

MOTHER. I don't want to know why!!!

MARY. I've kept it a secret...

MOTHER. Good! I don't want to know your secret! Keep it to yourself! if you tell it to me, it won't be a secret!

MARY. But I want to tell you... I think I've been trying for years to tell you...

MOTHER. What was this terrible thing I wanted for you! The blanket, the security of marriage – of belonging, of having a place in the sun, of being loved and wanted by the world. NOT TO BE A FREAK!

TAMMY. *(entering)* Why did you put her in the hospital? You knew she hated hospitals!

MARY. Tammy, you make no sense! She was old. She had a stroke. I had to put her in the hospital!

TAMMY. She had the stroke after you put her in the hospital. That's what gave her the stroke.

MOTHER. Cele... help me out... don't let them keep me here...

(SHE exits.)

MARY. *(to Danny)* Yes. That's true, isn't it? That's why they put her on a respirator. No, no, that's not why. She had the stroke because they had her on the respirator. Is that it? Which came first, the respirator or the stroke?

DANNY. It doesn't really matter now.

MARY. She hated the hospital. Why did I leave her there?

DANNY. She was too sick.

MARY. I thought, okay, okay, maybe she should be dead. Yes, yes, I thought that. Maybe the time had come, a time to weep, a time to die, all those times, you know –

(Mother leaves)

DANNY. There was nothing you could do.

MARY. That's what I did. Nothing.

DANNY. Mary – that number you gave me...

MARY. Number? What number?

DANNY. Seven-one-eight. Five-four-eight...

MARY. Four-oh-five-six. Yes! I must call it!

DANNY. I did call it.

MARY. You did?

DANNY. Yes. It isn't your mother's number.

MARY. Ah. *(thinks)* Well. *(thinks)* My mother's dead. *(thinks)* Somebody else must live there.

DANNY. Yes. She's here now.

MARY. Really? Who?

DANNY. Maybe you know.

> *(HE opens the door. LIZ KRUGER enters. SHE looks good, nice dress, heels. SHE pauses at the door)*

MARY. *(recognition is not far away. She points her finger at KRU)* Ah. Don't tell me.

> *(Holds her head and walks around the room. KRU just stands and waits)*

Of course I know you. You're looking extremely well. That's not to say you didn't always look well.

KRU. I wanted to…

MARY. *(holds up a hand as she continues to pace)* No, no, don't tell me. But your voice. I know that, too. Yes. I know that, too.

> *(casting glances at her)*

Yes, you're looking well. Neat. So neat. It's refreshing to look at you. Eyes clear, rested, bright, healthy. Why not, you did your five hundred mile jog before breakfast, eh? Yes, I know you.

> *(stops pacing)*

Kruger. You're Lizzie Kruger.

KRU. Yes.

MARY. Kru… Kru. How are you? I've been meaning to call you.

KRU. That's all right.

MARY. I keep going to the phone – then I don't know. I don't have change… or I can't remember your number… or your name…

KRU. Don't worry about it.

MARY. It's like a nightmare. I try so hard to call you... something always interferes.

KRU. Well... look. I'm here now.

MARY. Yes.

KRU. I'm sorry I didn't come sooner... but of course, I had no way of knowing you were... ill... or where you were.

MARY. No. How could you?

KRU. I didn't know what happened. You disappeared – just dropped off the face of the earth. I tried to find you. It was incredible – there wasn't a trace of you –

MARY. When was that? When did we see each other last?

KRU. Well... your mother had just died...

MARY. Yes. We worried about having to put her someplace – a home, a hospice. It was a terrible dilemma. But she made it easy for us. She died. Yes. She was always so thoughtful. So, Kru. Tell me about yourself. Where are you living now?

KRU. Oh, I'm still living in the same place.

MARY. Yes?

(**KRU** *looks at her. But clearly* **MARY** *doesn't know*)

KRU. Riverdale. I wanted to stay there – in case you came back.

MARY. Ah. And what are you doing with yourself?

KRU. Well, I finally got my doctorate.

MARY. You did? Well, good for you! And where are you living now?

(**KRU** *is enormously startled.* **MARY** *is so obviously sincere that for a moment,* **KRU** *cannot speak*)

KRU. *(finally, softly)* Riverdale.

MARY. Ah, yes, of course. In that beautiful apartment. With a swimming pool. *(hesitates)* There is a swimming pool, isn't there?

KRU. Yes. On the roof.

MARY. I love to swim.

KRU. I know you do.

> (**KRU** *glances tentatively at* **DANNY**. *He gives her a barely imperceptible nod*)

Do you… do you remember the last time we were at my place, Celia?

MARY. The last time. Well. I don't know. Let me see.

KRU. You came for dinner…

MARY. Yes, yes, of course! You cooked. It was wonderful.

> (*and she abruptly stops*)

DANNY. Yes? Go on?

MARY. (*turning to him*) What?

DANNY. What was wonderful?

MARY. Oh. The dinner. Kru is such a good cook.

DANNY. Then? Then what happened?

MARY. I don't know.

DANNY. You don't know? What about Tammy? Did she come? Was Tammy there?

MARY. Tammy?

DANNY. Your daughter. You remember her, don't you?

> (*Music begins.*)

TRIO.
> WHEN I HEAR THAT SERENADE IN BLUE
> I'M SOMEWHERE IN ANOTHER WORLD…
> ALONE WITH YOU…

MARY. Don't make a big thing out of it. It wasn't important!

DANNY. Then let's hear it.

KRU. Dance with me.

TRIO.
> SHARING ALL THE DREAMS
> WE USED TO KNOW
> MANY MOONS AGO…

DANNY. I know you remember. What happened that night at Kru's?

KRU. Dance with me. It's all right. Come on, Cecilia. Dance with me.

TRIO.

>   ONCE AGAIN YOUR FACE
>   COMES BACK TO ME...

DANNY. What happened?

MARY. I – don't – know!

DANNY. You just said it! There was music playing. She asked you to dance. Then something happened. What?

MARY. I told you! I told you! I forgot!

DANNY. You forgot? *(exploding)* Okay, then! Forget it! Forget everything! Forget me! Forget I ever existed!

MARY. Oh, go away! Leave me alone!

DANNY. Sure, I'll leave you alone! Delete, erase, cancel. It never happened! None of it ever happened! There was never a Noel to take you to the prom. Never a mother who taught you how to make coffee. And your daughter? Tammy? A fairy tale! Never existed!

MARY. Are you crazy? Of course she existed!

DANNY. You just made her up. The child you always wanted. You never had her!

MARY. Yes! I had her! I had her!

KRU. Dance with me.

DANNY. A product of your imagination!

MARY. That's a lie!

KRU. It's all right. Come on, Cecilia. Dance with me.

DANNY. Not if you don't remember. If you don't remember, it never happened!

TRIO.

>   JUST LIKE THE THEME
>   OF SOME FORGOTTEN MELODY...

>   *(Mary steps into Kru's arms. They dance slowly.)*

KRU. It's all right. It's all right.

TRIO.

>   IN THE ALBUM OF MY MEMORY...

KRU. Don't you want to stay? Don't you want to be with me?

MARY. Oh, Kru. It's all I want.

(Kru takes Mary's face in her hands. Slowly turns it to hers. Tammy enters. Mary senses something. Abruptly turns. Sees her.)

TAMMY. Wow.

MARY. Oh, God.

TAMMY. I guess you didn't expect me.

MARY. Tammy – I thought you were…

(Kru walks over to Danny, stands by him.)

TAMMY. You don't have to leave, Kru. I'm the one who's leaving.

MARY. No, don't go. Here, sit down, let me fix you a plate…

TAMMY. What I mean is I'm leaving for college. Remember?

MARY. Well, of course, but you can still have…

TAMMY. I'll be at that out of town college you're so hell-bent on my going to.

MARY. I'm so hell-bent? What's so terrible about…

TAMMY. I guess this is why you wanted to give up our apartment.

MARY. Please, darling, let me get you dinner…

TAMMY. I guess you'll move in here with Kru. Such a neat place Kru has. Giant TV, great sound system, that fabulous terrace, loads of books – everything you love.

MARY. Well, my first priority is you…

TAMMY. Me? But I'll be in Chicago. I'll be away at school.

MARY. Well, you'll be home for vacation…

TAMMY. Right. I'll be home for vacation. But what then? Won't I be in the way?

MARY. In the way? Don't be ridiculous. We can do things together. You want to go riding with Kru, rock- climbing…

TAMMY. Oh, stop! Don't make me part of your little intrigue!

MARY. Don't say that!

TAMMY. Why not?

MARY. Because you know Kru loves you!

TAMMY. Yes, once upon a time. That's when she was my friend! Now she's yours!

MARY. She's our friend!

TAMMY. Bullshit!

MARY. That's enough! You can just cut it out, okay!

TAMMY. Cut it out? Cut what out, Mom? Me? Sure, let's cut me out! Grandma's dead and now you can send me off! Does that suit you? Will that suit your plans?

MARY. Oh, go away, Tammy! Just go away! You're talking too much and you just don't understand…

TAMMY. What? What don't I understand?

MARY. You don't know what you're saying and you're driving me crazy! Go away! Go for a swim! Cool off!

TAMMY. Okay. I'll go for a swim.

MARY. Wait a minute…

TAMMY. Got to cool off.

MARY. Wait…

TAMMY. *(backing out)* A swim.

MARY. WAIT!!

TAMMY. A swim, a swim…

MARY. No! Wait! Wait! *(screaming)* NO!

(*Tammy is out. Danny rushes to Mary*)

DANNY. Okay! Okay! What happened? What happened to Tammy?

MARY. She didn't wait! She didn't wait!

DANNY. Yes! Then what happened? You remember, don't you?

MARY. Yes. She was on a respirator.

DANNY. That's your mother. And Tammy?

MARY. Yes, yes, I remember. You see, she had that terrible accident…

DANNY. Accident? Yes? What happened?

MARY. She fell off a horse.

DANNY. Fell off a horse?

MARY. Yes, she was out riding and… no, it wasn't a horse. She fell off a house.

DANNY. Fell off a house?

MARY. *(turns to* **KRU***)* That's right, isn't it, Kru?

KRU. *(in a whisper)* No…

DANNY. What about the accident?

MARY. Accident? Oh, yes! She was leaning against the railing of this house, the railing of the balcony, you see, and it gave way. And she fell off. And hit her head. The side of her head, right here, see?

DANNY. Is that what happened?

MARY. Yes. No. Wait a minute. I don't think that's what happened. Ah! I remember. She ate something…

DANNY. Ate something…

MARY. Yes, and it gave her a terrible time! I don't know, I suppose the mayonnaise went bad. That happens all the time. That's why you can't take tuna sandwiches to the beach. The beach! That's where it happened! She went in swimming immediately after lunch.

DANNY. *(going along with her)* And got a cramp.

MARY. Yes, but she loved the ocean. The waves crashing on the beach put her to sleep at night.

DANNY. Who? Who, Mary?

MARY. She just got sick. She had the vapors. She hated the hospital.

DANNY. Who, Mary? Who?

MARY. I held her in my arms. I had to keep her from slipping away. I said, "I love you. Only stay. Stay, Tammy. Stay."

(**DANNY** *waits. But* **MARY** *is not saying more.* **HE** *turns to* **KRU**.)

KRU. We found her on the pool steps. A bruise on the side of her head. She hit the steps when she dived in.

MARY. Stay, Tammy.

KRU. They took her to Columbia Presbyterian on a Hundred and Sixty-eighth Street.

DANNY. A Hundred and Sixty-eighth Street...

MARY. Stay, Tammy.

KRU. She was in a coma. They said it was irreversible. They needed Celia's consent to take her off life support.

MARY. Stay, Tammy.

KRU. She said she had to think about it. She would take a walk to think about it.

MARY. And a gurgle she gave. Oh, willow. Tit willow. Tit willow.

KRU. That's the last time I saw her.

(A moment. Then Kru gets up)

You know how to reach me.

(She looks at Mary. Exits. Mary watches her go)

MARY. I have to go, too.

DANNY. Where?

MARY. Oh, no place special. Just for a little walk. Maybe a run.

DANNY. A run? Well, you can stay here with me and we can work on getting you well. Or you can go on running. Only problem is when you come back, it will still be here. As real and shattering as the first time. Because every time you come back, it is the first time.

MARY. Now you don't have to leave. You just wait right here for me.

DANNY. It was a wish. A wish. A wish so awful you couldn't bear to consciously think it. *(carefully)* How easy it would be if they – just – weren't here.

(she stands still)

And it happened. It happened. The terrible wish came true. But you didn't make it happen.

*(**MOTHER** enters. **MARY** turns to look at her.)*

MOTHER. Nothing like a good cup of coffee!

DANNY. When bad things happen, the pain is crushing. We think we can't go on. But somehow, we go on. We think we'll never get over it. But somehow, we get over it. The pain fades. The healing begins.

(*NOEL enters*)

NOEL. I'll tell you my secret if you tell me yours.

MARY. Will you please open this door?

DANNY. My wife's name was Cathy. I was planning to leave her. But she died. And all I have left is the memory. Memories don't have to be sad. Memories are the proof of our existence. Memories are what we are.

(*Danny walks to the door. Unlocks it. Walks back to the table. Mary walks to the door. She opens it.*)

So now you know. You are Cecilia Schooner. I am Doctor Lucchesi. Now we can mourn. We can cry and we can scream and we can tear our hair out in our agony. But we can stop running.

(*Danny sits down at the table.*)

It's time to wake up. Everybody's waiting. The birds. The sun. The day. Nothing can get started till you get up.

(*TAMMY walks in.*)

TAMMY. If you buy a box, Mom – at least I'll have sold one. Will you buy at least one?

(*Mary looks at her.*)

MARY. Of course I will, darling. I'll buy a whole bunch.

(*She closes the door and walks back into the room. She sits down at the table with Danny. He drops the keys on the table.*)

(*LIGHTS FADE*)

(*CURTAIN*)

COSTUMES

MOTHER

Act I:
Panty hose, scuffs, pink dress, overdress robe, shoes, purse, shawl, and apron.

Act II:
Salmon dress and jacket, Act I shoes, Act I overdress robe, winter dress and sweater.

MARY

Act I:
Tan slacks, socks, bandages, shirt, clogs. T-shirt top, brown skirt, jog pants, jacket, socks and sneakers.

ZELDA

Act I:
Animal print suit, purse, panty hose, shoes, earrings, watch, blue dress and jacket, second pair of earrings.

Act II:
Navy dress and jacket, shoes, Act I purse, Act I jewelry.

TAMMY

Act I:
Green skirt, Girl Scout blouse, Girl Scout sash, socks, sneakers, red camp shirt, tan shorts, jeans, shirt, and jacket.

Act II:
Jeans and T-shirt top, hooded sweatshirt, Act 1 Girl Scout outfit.

KRU

Act I:
Navy slacks, striped shirt, flats, socks, red shirt, tan slacks, sneakers, jeans, pink shirt, navy slacks, shirt, and red blazer.

Act II:
Paisley slacks, aqua top, flats, knee-high socks, polka-dot dress, jacket, panty hose, and heels.

NOEL

Act I:
Painted jeans, shirt, sneakers, socks, bathing suit, T-shirt top, flip-flops, tuxedo, blacks socks, shirt, bow tie, cummerbund.

Act II:
Shorts, shirt, red turtleneck, jeans, toggle coat, and scarf.

DR. OLEANDER

Act I:
Suit, suspenders, tie, white-collar striped shirt, black socks, wing-tip shoes, khaki pants, "Hopkins" sweatshirt or plaid button down shirt, belt, loafers.

Act II:
White shirt, Act I suit pants, sweater vest, second tie, Act I wing-tip shoes, camel jacket, third tie, blue shirt, fourth tie.

DANNY

Act I:
Jeans, belt, socks, boots, black T-shirt top, check jacket.

Act II:
Act I costume can be repeated.

FURNITURE

Bed
Table (Kitchen Size)
3 Chairs
Small Refrigerator

PROPERTIES

PROP	CHARACTER
Clipboard w/Papers/Folder	Oleander
Tape Recorder	Oleander
Coffee Cup	Mother
Coffee Maker	Mother
Paint Can	Noel
Paint Brush	Noel
Cd's	Danny
Girl Scout Cookie Boxes	Tammy
A Book	Zelda
Paper Bag Of Cookies	Zelda
Gift Box With Jogging Suit	Danny
Bag w/ Socks, Running shoes & Pedometer	Danny
Beach Towel	Noel
Wicker Picnic Basket	Kru
Thermos (In Basket)	Kru
Blanket, Glasses, Bread (In Basket)	Kru
Badminton Racket And Cock	Tammy
Cassette Player (In Basket)	Kru
Corsage In A Box	Noel
Cell Phone	Danny
Set Of Keys	Danny
Ice Pack	Oleander
Phone	Danny
A Plastic Basin	Kru
Rocks Glass (A Vermouth Cassis)	Kru
Vase	Mother
Records/Cd's	Zelda
Scarf	Mary
2 Brandy Snifters (With Brandy)	Kru/Mary

From the Reviews of **FUGUE**...

"*FUGUE* IS FASCINATING! It casts a dreamy, mysterious spell over its audience."
- *Cleveland News Herald*

"Remarkable and Poignant Theatre!"
- *Syrcause Post Standard*

"A Fascinating and Entertaining new play!"
- WMNR Radio

"An INSPIRING AND DEEPLY UPLIFTING PLAY! Theatre at its finest touches the very pulse of life, and *Fugue* does so brilliantly!"
- *Watertown Daily Times*

"Winner of the American Theatre Critics Awards for Dest Play in Regional Theatre, *Fugue* is a masterpiece... This piece is as charming as it is terrifying, as honest as it is dark, intriguing as it is engaging."
- *UK Theatre Network*

"...the play is surprisingly effective adn ultimately moving."
- *Theatermania*

"...a must see."
- Dr. Joy Brown, WWOR Radio

"...a most interesting play... an exploration of a rare but intriguing emotional disorder..."
- Jane E. Brody, *New York Times*

"With its potent blend of wit and tragedy, Lee Thuna's *Fugue* succeeds where many attempts to dramatize the therapeutic process have failed... Long after its final refrain, *Fugue*'s poignant meditation on loss grief and guilt continue to resonate."
- *Show Business*

ABOUT THE PLAYWRIGHT

LEE THUNA - PLAYS: *What's Left?* 10-minute Play Festival, Cherry Lane Theatre. *Fugue,* produced at the Cherry Lane Theatre, NYC. Regional theatre productions: Long Wharf, Syracuse Stage, Cleveland Play House. Winner of the American Theatre Critics Award for Best Play in Regional Theatre.

Broadway Plays: *The Natural Look,* with Brenda Vaccaro, Gene Hackman, Jerry Orbach, Doris Roberts, *Let Me Hear You Smile* with Sandy Dennis and James Broderick, *Show Me Where the Good Times Are* (Book).

Regional Theatre: *Frazzled,* Victory Theatre, *Dr. Jekyll & Mr. Hyde* (Book), Goodspeed Opera House, La Mirada Music Theatre, Hermosa Playhouse. *The Eleventh* (Book) Fort Lauderdale, Florida, *Love From Mother,* Lambertville Tent, *A House for Rosie,* Mark Taper Lab.

FILM (TV): Maya Angelou's *I Know Why the Caged Bird Sings,** *Family Secrets** with Stefanie Powers, Melissa Gilbert, James Spader, Maureen Stapleton. *Judith Kratz' Torch Song* with Rachel Welch.

TELEVISION: Created and produced *The Goodtime Girls* (ABC) and *The Natural Look* (CBS). Writer/Producer: *Angie, Grandpa Goes to Washington.* Writer: *Lou Grant,* * *Family, In the Beginning.*

* WGA nominations for Best Teleplay.

BOOKS: *The Baby Book* (with Saint Subber) and *Debby Gold, NYPD.*

Member of the Dramatists Guild, Writers Guild of America West, League of Professional Theatre Women.

Also by
Lee Thuna...

The Natural Look

Let Me Hear You Smile

Show Me Where
The Good Times Are

OTHER TITLES AVAILABLE FROM SAMUEL FRENCH

THE NATURAL LOOK

Lee Thuna

Comedy / 4m, 2f / Int.

The scenes are set in the Park Avenue apartment of Reedy and Bernie Harris, and the glamorous office of Contessa Cosmetics, Inc., where Reedy is advertising director. At the moment, Reedy finds herself involved in a power play with Malcolm, her assistant who was hired by Contessa's eccentric owner, the Countess. Reedy is faced with another problem when Jane, her husband's former flame, arrives for the dinner party - and takes over. She is a compulsive homemaker who likes nothing better than to cook, clean and be a housewife. It also seems she would like nothing better than Bernie. Feeling that she is losing her job to Malcolm and her husband to Jane, Reedy decides to quit the job she loves and devote herself to being a full-time housewife. But, on the one hand, Malcolm is unmasked by the Countess as a spy for a competitor, and is fired; and, on the other, Bernie reveals that the last thing in the world he wants is to have her hang around the house the way his mother did. Happily, Reedy can have her job - and her husband.